WE ARE GREMBLING

WE ARE GREEN AND TREMBLING

Gabriela Cabezón Cámara

translated from the Spanish by Robin Myers

A NEW DIRECTIONS
PAPERBOOK ORIGINAL

Excerpts from *Don Quixote by Miguel de Cervantes: A New Translation
by Edith Grossman* copyright © 2003 by Edith Grossman
and used by permission of HarperCollins Publishers

First published by New Directions in 2025 as NDP1635
Manufactured in the United States of America

Library of Congress Cataloging-in-Publication Data
Names: Cabezón Cámara, Gabriela, 1968– author. |
Myers, Robin, 1987– translator.
Title: We are green and trembling / Gabriela Cabezón Cámara ;
translated by Robin Myers.
Other titles: Niñas del naranjel. English
Description: New York : New Directions Publishing, 2025.
Identifiers: LCCN 2024059018 | ISBN 9780811238618 (paperback) |
ISBN 9780811238625 (ebook)
Subjects: LCGFT: Novels.
Classification: LCC PQ7798.413.A3 N5613 2025 |
DDC 863/.7—dc23/eng/20241212
LC record available at https://lccn.loc.gov/2024059018

2 4 6 8 10 9 7 5 3 1

New Directions Books are published for James Laughlin
by New Directions Publishing Corporation
80 Eighth Avenue, New York 10011

For Abril Schaerer

For María Moreno

For my loving pack

WE ARE GREEN AND TREMBLING

1

My beloved aunt,

I am as innocent and forged in the image and likeness of God as any other, as every other, though I have been a cabin boy, shopkeeper, and soldier, and before then, long before, a small girl at your skirts. "Daughter," "little daughter," so did you call me, and not even now, not even with my martial shoulders and my mustache and my calloused sword-wielding hands, would you think to describe me otherwise. Dear aunt, I would ask you if I could, are you still alive? For I believe you are, and I believe you are waiting to bestow upon me what is yours, what was ours; the convent of Saint Sebastián el Antiguo, whose construction was commanded by your grandfather, the father of the father of my father, the Marquis Don Sebastián Erauso y Pérez Errázuriz de Donostia. Give it to some other girl, and, I beg of you, pray do keep reading these words.

You must know that I've become a teller of tales, and that I carry things to and fro, for I am a muleteer, which I suspect will surprise you. And I sing, and, should the need arise along the way, I hunt, and I arrive and deliver my cargo, which is not my own, as the cargo of a muleteer is never his own, and I collect my coins and return to doing what I wish; I behold the trees and vines, the long and flexible roots of the air; they become a net, like the nets cast by fishermen, or no, like webs spun by spiders, rather, throngs of spiders engrossed in their weaving, some above and some below and some within the others, oh, green and vast and aquiver, aquiver like all living things, my beloved, like you and I and all the plants, like the lizards and the entire jungle, which, as I must tell you again and again until you understand, is an animal made of many others. It cannot be

3

traversed on foot as people do; there are no paths or straight lines, the jungle makes its clay of you, it shapes you with its own shape, and now you fly, an insect, you clamber, a monkey, you slither, a snake. As you can see, it is not so strange that I, once your beloved little girl, should be today your firstborn American son; no longer the prioress you dreamed of, nor the noble fruit of the noble seed of our lineage, your little girl is now a respected muleteer, a man of peace. And in the jungle, a creature of two, three, or four legs alongside the others, who are mine as I am theirs, a creature, after all, that darts up and down and scales and encloses and leaps and swings on vines and tipples the poisonous venom of the voracious tendrils and the tiny flowers with petals so fragile that they can scarcely weather the faintest breeze, buckling under the weight of mere droplets, for all things are always dripping here, and the butterflies—how you would love the sight of them!—as large as the fist of a large man, larger than my own hands, larger than my soldier hands, beloved aunt; for did you know I have been named a second lieutenant and strung with medals? Yet that was not in the jungle …

"Hey, che, who do you speak to, stranger, Yvypo Amboae?"

"Antonio. My name is Antonio. I come from distant lands, not strange ones. These lands are strange. And I wasn't speaking but writing, Mitākuña."

"You are strange, che. All day talking and talking, reñe'ẽ, reñe'ẽ, reñe'ẽ, talking to yourself."

"Mba'érepa?"

"What was that, Michī?"

"She asks you why, why do you talk to yourself."

"I am writing a letter to my aunt. Look, you two, this is a quill, this is ink, and these are words. Would you like to hear them?"

"I hear you for hours. Lies you speak, Yvypo Amboae, lies to your aunt. Where is your aunt?"

"Far away, in Spain. Be still a while, Mitākuña, and let me keep writing. Yet that was not in the jungle ..."

... that is a story I will tell you in time, dear aunt. Let me tell you now about the fragrances of the forest, which are strong as the spirits soldiers drink, as village rotgut, and about the other flowers, mammoth and fleshy and carnivorous, nearly beasts, for here in the jungle the animals bloom and the plants bite, and I believe I have even seen them walking, I swear this to you, and leaping, for vines do leap; all things seethe here, whereas the forest rustles, as well you know; I remember your attention to the presence of the fox, with its faint rustle of leaves in your forest, and to the bear, with its heavy rustle of trunks and branches; the forest rustles, but not the jungle, the jungle seethes, full of eyes; life surges inside it as lava surges in volcanoes, as if the lava were trees and birds and mushrooms and monkeys and coatis and coconuts and snakes and ferns and caimans and tigers and trumpet trees and fish and vipers and palms and rivers and fronds, and all other things within it were amalgams of these primary ones.

The jungle is a volcano, beloved aunt, a volcano in eternal eruption, slow, very slow, an eruption that does not kill, that brings forth green and pulses green water welling from the soil of my forest that in no way belongs to me, but I to it, and is nothing like the forest, nothing at all, dear aunt; jungle, wild jungle, this jungle of mine, much like the distant jungles of your stories, yes, but you should see it, you should smell it, and you would make it yours and take of it as I have done, and oh, if you could touch the stalks and petals and enormous leaves and furred vermin and colors, for here colors can be touched, how pale your Donostian rainbow by comparison, verily spectral in the chill mists, but not here; here colors are flesh, because all things are flesh in this jungle, where I dwell in the company of my animals and my servants, they belong to me, just as I, first girl, then boy, was yours, and the forest was ours in our Donostia when I was but a maiden, my most beloved aunt.

"Yvy mombyry, far away. She will not hear you. What is aunt?"

"Of course she cannot hear me now. She'll hear me when my letter arrives, Mitākuña."

"Mba'érepa?"

"Look, Michī: these drawings are words. They will travel on a ship and on a horse and then reach her hands someday. An aunt is the sister of your father or of your mother."

"Mba'érepa?"

"Now what did she ask?"

"Why, she says."

"Why what."

"Why is your aunt the sister of my father or my mother."

"No, no, she is the sister of *a* father or *a* mother."

"Mba'érepa?"

"Because they are siblings. Would you like some oranges?"

"What are oranges, Yvypo Amboae?"

"Sweet, acidic fruits, orange as the wings of that butterfly."

"Pindó fruits, che."

"No, Mitākuña. Oranges are the size of my fist."

"Mba'érepa?"

"Because they are, Michī, because that is how they are. Just as you are small and have two eyes, little one. Time for us to go."

"Nahániri."

"She says no, che."

"And why is that?"

"Why what."

"Why not."

"Because she does not want."

"Look, the monkeys will ride on my back and the little horse must walk. Would you like to ride on the big horse, Michī?"

6

"Naháñiri."

"Then you must ride on my back. Since you are only strong enough to breathe and speak two words."

"Mba'érepa oranges?"

"So you have learned a new word, Michī! Because I made a promise to the Virgin. You must wonder who and what a virgin is. All right, all right. We're not going anywhere. Stay here, you two, and you take care of her, Mitākuña. You are the eldest. The mare and the colt will stay and protect you, worry not. I must go with the monkeys and your dog in search of oranges, and later, as we eat, I will tell you all about the Lady. About the Virgin, I mean."

They walk: the monkeys clutching Antonio's back with what's left of their strength. The dog, Red, springing about, her little reddish body sometimes swallowed into the bright green ferns, sometimes flying brown on brown over the enormous roots or among the taut weave of the vines. The horses, stalled by thickets every two strides. Antonio slowly making his way, clearing a path with his sword, afraid of blunting its edge. He blunts it.

They find no orange groves, only palms and more palms, long and pliable, towering palo santo trees, and animals whose only detectable sound is the foliage parting or reuniting with their steps. The occasional song, the occasional growl. They retrace their steps. Red panting with her tongue out and Antonio carrying the monkeys in his arms: they can't grip his back any longer. The mosquitoes bite and bite until they're numb. The girls fall asleep on the cape he spread out on the ground. The mare and the colt stand guard, heads bowed toward them. He sets down the monkeys by the girls. The girls are so small, their ribs protruding, their tiny arms like sticks. Their small faces angular with hunger. Their eyes enormous, sockets honed and ghostly. They're two tiny skeletons covered in skin, straining to breathe. The older girl barely comes up to Antonio's thigh. The younger, to his knee. A great yellow-streaking star protects them all with blue and orange light. Antonio takes it as a good omen: maybe it heralds a rebirth. They need one. So does he. He's spent. His body subject to the rhythm of the others. He can no longer remember why he's protecting them. They have their charms, but he'd be better off alone: he could write uninterrupted. Leave at whim. Eat when he was hungry. Sleep the whole night through. As soon as he comes across an Indian, he'll hand them over. Why should he risk his neck for a pair of urchins, monkeys, horses, and a dog? And a sword, but this he has forgotten. As he has forgotten that his neck was already at risk. Protecting the Indian girls was a promise he made to his Virgin of the Orange Grove. Not long ago, she'd saved his life on a wing and a prayer: the breadth of a hair. It was the Lady. Maybe. He's not sure he believes this anymore. Or that he doesn't. Much less that he no longer needs his Virgin. So he'd better keep his promises; he got off on the wrong foot, after all. He failed her twice. Two days in a row. He only needs to keep giving water to the girls. And writing to his aunt. It isn't much. He wonders if the mosquitoes have been joined by barigüí flies, which gnaw more than bite. He'd better build a fire. And a shelter. He takes the captain's sword and cuts some fronds and right away he weaves them through the vines and the palo santo trunk. It's the tallest tree in sight. That's why he chose it. Besides, it's ringed by palms. One can walk a bit. And see what's around. It isn't bad, this little palm hut. He builds the fire inside it. Maybe then the biting will stop. He arranges the girls and monkeys close to the heat. The dog joins them. The horses stand, nibbling ferns and swishing their tails, too short to swat the mosquitoes and the barigüís. Nothing is enough. The palo santo boughs fill the air with sweet perfume. It's beautiful. He coughs at once: too much smoke. Better find dry wood. First he rereads what he's written to his aunt. He sees that it is good. He gets up singing.

... craved all of them in sight ...

He hadn't known that he was so keen on the jungle or that he still harbored any fondness for his aunt. Or even that he was a muleteer.

Oh blind man, tell me, blind man ...

But he feels a stone in his throat: maybe there's some truth in what he's written. For the jungle has its marvels, the prioress her happy memories, and he has cargo to deliver.

Would you an orange give ...

He's content. Two days ago, however, he'd been brooding, tucked into a fold of himself. He was terrified. That he would drown in the shit of the dungeon before the rope choked off his breath. That he would be buried in filth and rags. That he would thus be resurrected as a beggar, in body and soul.

2

From the vulture's perspective, the barracks are a banquet. Built on the highest point of the cliffs by the river. Flanked by constructions in two parallel lines. The army chapel, the bishop's house, the captain general's house, and the soldiers' quarters. On the other side, the arsenal, the shop, the dungeons, and the shacks where the Indians live divided by sex. The best part, deliciously fragrant, is the middle: the large bare plaza, two hundred paces wide, the only treeless spot in sight from up above. The barracks are a patch of cleared earth cracking in the sun. The scene, a laden platter. The vulture, indifferent to the ash and bones, is most attentive to the bonfire, and the gallows. The man—face lined with scars, fine lips, nearly neckless, back strong if slightly buckled, stout callused hands, short legs, sharp nose—hadn't sensed the bird gliding over the barracks as easily as he himself would amble toward a tavern. If he could amble. Only the plaza was visible from the cell, the bonfire dwindling on that rainy afternoon. And the gallows as his only exit. Antonio was suffering. A Spanish gentleman couldn't die this way, like some wretched beggar. No fine sword, no silk doublet. What fate awaits a person who enters the beyond in such a way? Because apart from being, one must seem. Both on earth and in heaven. And what would become of him, unfit as he was for a servant's latrine? He would only leave this cell on his way to the noose after confession. Everything hurt. The shackles on his wrists and ankles. His fellow prisoners. Rough peasants, revolting rustics one and all. The threads of the coarse cloth that clad them. The tremors of mangled prayers. The insults they shouted. And the weeping of the little girls. The humiliation of dying on the same roster as such beasts. The cacophony. Each and every noise: the farts, the snores, the sobs, and farther off, the military shouts, the bustle of the soldiers. In the distance, birds cawing. The jaguars roaring. The insects shrilling. The rhythm of the toads. And the faint furrow in the air, sliced by the vulture overhead. The river's ebb. It was all folded together, and it was, the whole of it, a lacerating wound. Injured even by the air, even by the softest voice, he plumbed each instant for a door. A silence wrested him from himself, flung him out into the world. Hope numbed the pain: what was that muffled shriek? Searing ice! And he threw himself against the bars.

Then he saw them. The Indians. Bound. Surrounded by sabers, harquebuses, and torches. They feared the fire. And the bishop, who blessed the rotten flesh that would be stuffed into their mouths. Flesh from the cows that those same Indians had killed the week before. The prelate didn't clarify that the cows could've been killed by other Indians: they were all the same. Perhaps it was those who sat fettered there. Perhaps not. Nothing about their skeletal frames suggested a recent roast. But the terror was theirs. If they opened their mouths, they'd die of indigestion. Or disgust. And if they didn't, they'd be whisked off to the colossal pyre, rekindled now. Just in case. And because the fire was dying. Torrential, the rain. The bonfire too, forever gobbling down trees and people. It is the fire of God, everyone says, and they must be right, for such are the wages of heretics, Indians, and Jews. Not long ago, they found a Jewish man around these parts. He was at home, surrounded by candelabra, singing Lord knows what in his devilish Christ-murdering tongue. They burned him, his ten children, and his wife. The whole village went to watch the blaze. They don't watch the Indians, though. Who are legion and burn every day.

They were melting, the Indians. What a spectacle! Antonio had forgotten about the cell, the gallows, and his pungent companions: he was too afraid of dying like a villain. The bishop and the captain deliberated gravely by the bonfire. At last, unable to agree, they resigned themselves. They concluded that it would not be possible to kindle one Indian at a time, or even two or three at a time, in compliance with custom and procedure. After all, they simply melted down in the heat. They were all stuck together. They'd have to lift the molten Indians by the edges and set them directly onto the fire. It was urgent:

"They are escaping, monsignor. One cannot ever know with certainty that he has finished slaying. Lord forgive me, your illustriousness, yet I cannot deny that there is always something left alive in them. Strike and strike and some Indian remnant nonetheless rises up once more. Curses!"

A hundred soldiers began to haul the wood. Some of their hands caught fire, and instead of snuffing these resolute embers, they leapt into the pink, waxy lagoon of white skeletons, like stiff trees in a saltpeter bed. Until there was nothing left. It was the Spaniards who burned. Their bodies gave fire to the fire, and their movement kept the blaze from going out. They crackled. They burned far better than the Indians. The captain made a mental note of his soldiers' combustion: he might run out of firewood before he ran out of men.

"Valiant warriors of Christ," the bishop remarked to the captain, which brightened the mood.

The prelate sang last rites, his right hand fluttering pyre-ward, smiling like a piranha, his left foot sliding in graceful little steps, his flesh undulating beneath his garments, which were embroidered with precious stones and gold. Rippling in the eddies of the hot breeze yielded by the flames, he opted for an extreme unction of broad address:

"Ut a peccatis liberatum te salvet atque propitius allevet. Amen, amen, amen, amen to each and every one of you, my children."

The captain, short and straight and sturdy as a peg, flung silver medallions with red and white and yellow ribbons and howled postmortem promotions:

"Go with God, Second Lieutenant Diéguez! May God keep you in his glory, Sergeant Rivero! May your resurrection be swift, Captain Bermúdez! My dear fellows, my valorous soldiers."

He crooned to them in death, his chest aflame. The captain general was moved. Slowly, he went quiet. He wasn't sure how many postmortem promotions he was allowed to grant per year or how many he'd already granted or how many were still available, if any. Let's see: there was a total of one thousand per year and he had already granted eight hundred. Or it was one thousand per lustrum. Or per decade. Something to do with a thousand. He had squandered hundreds, he was certain, on the occasions of the Cimarron uprising and the Inca scions' revolt. Hundreds: he couldn't remember how many, but he thought of poor Fernández, losing his leanness and his soldier's bearing, hunched for years over a desk, soliciting pensions from the governor, the viceroy, and the king. Poor Fernández. And poor widows and orphans who must still be petitioning for what they were owed. So it was a thousand and he'd granted eight hundred. Or it was eight hundred and he had granted a thousand. What did it matter? They wouldn't see so much as a doubloon in the end. But it did matter: a soldier must be just and measured. So, eight hundred and a thousand. Or seven hundred and nine hundred thirty-one. He got his numbers and his thoughts all muddled. And he couldn't ask anyone because his secretary had been set ablaze as well. He didn't understand why Fernández had flung himself into the flames. He wasn't a man

13

of faith. The captain had always suspected he was neither really a Catholic nor named Fernández. But he was a fine secretary, so he didn't wring his hands over the details. God loves those who labor tirelessly for the proclamation across the realm of the Good News, the Birth, the Death, and the Resurrection of His Son, he told himself, and relaxed. What had come over Fernández, throwing himself into the conflagration? The lukewarm sweetness that the ember soldiers had kindled in his heart was suddenly doused: who had authorized Fernández to immolate himself? He didn't know how else to make his will be done. Nor was he so sure what his will really was, but his gaze remained steady and strong. Vexed and silent, he clattered in place like a spinning top of silver-plated armor. Fernández on the pyre, that imbecile. A fried egg, an idiotic moth clinging to the flame, a pine cone without a scent of pine, a nothing, Fernández, incinerating in a blaze that didn't need him as fodder. By contrast, he, his superior, his captain general, needed a secretary to tell him what to do with his own words, which, as they well knew, he and Fernández and all the rest, plunge into the world with the full weight of law and force. Not to be forgotten as easily as the words of all that good-for-nothing riffraff, burned or hanged each day, blubbering nonsense, because—well, in any case, who cared. He could always grant plots of land, it's true, but what good land remained unconquered, and what had become of his zeal for conquering? He was weary of land and gold, and all he wanted was to leave this savage world behind. But where would he go, and with whose permission. And why all the fuss, when all was said and done, just for a few famished degenerates, nursing the hunger of many lives, of fathers and grandfathers, of great-great-grandfathers and great-great-great-grandsons. A bunch of breadless, toothless fools, his men. Some were already accustomed to going hungry. He was astonished yet again by the Conquest of the New World. A feat performed by a handful of malnourished wretches who couldn't obey, couldn't even await an order, and leapt into the flames without one such as himself, who had descended from generations upon generations of well-fed, decent folk, granting his permission. Martyrdom and disobedience, the captain thought. His eyes reddened. He stilled his top and stopped listening, smelling, and nearly seeing altogether.

The bishop, a hulking cherub, sought the captain's eyes and leaned in with his blond curls halo-ringing his pink face. He didn't want to lose, he thought, the only other gentleman in the entire barracks who was capable of singing Biscayne lullabies late at night, after the wine, mired in melancholy at finding himself so far from home. This extraordinary toast—in broad daylight, facing the bonfire—rescued the captain from his lethargy. Relieved by the invitation that extracted him from his impossible accounts—how many promotions had he granted, for the love of Christ?—the soldier reacted with elation, practically soaring, plucked by Bacchus from the swampy labyrinth of imperial bureaucracy, which was so twisted that it could've been invented by pederast scribes for the sole purpose of weakening the virile administration of the force and justice befitting a soldier, a captain, a nobleman. He decided to set aside all bureaucratic affairs for later. He'd have to find a new secretary. Some effeminate sort who would take pleasure in fussing over laws and norms and articles and exceptions and prebends so that the numbers would add up properly. Or, even better, he'd have a long chat with the bishop and ask which held more weight in the judgment of God—and of men, his only real interest, and with respect to the ember soldiers—martyrdom or disobedience? And if it would be His will that a captain general should honor words uttered to insubordinate men-at-arms, even if they were martyrs. If it was possible to be both martyred and insubordinate at once. Or didn't God, Lord of Armies, wish there to be captains and soldiers; did He not want some to give orders and have others obey? Later, better wait till later. He smiled, swilled a little wine, then a little more, and felt reborn, the conquering force of his body, and with it he brought chalice against chalice once more. Gold clinked, stones clanked. Wine sloshed onto the face of the bishop, who laughed purply. An Indian girl appeared out of thin air with a length of white linen in one hand and a bowl of water in the other. Ten small skeletal forms rushed to serve them some more, pouring meticulously to spare their lordly robes from spatter. One tripped and stained his military doublet. The bishop perked up: in a single gesture—red, his angelic face; swift, his slap—he hurled the man into the fire with his own two hands. The man screamed and burned.

"Hurrah! A new Christian, good fellow!"
"Praise be to God, dear bishop."

3

I remember you, beloved aunt; your splendid white locks, when nightly you freed them from their black veil to illume your cell like the luster of a mountain spring as it tumbles into the forest. Your eyes like a Biscay winter sky, stern blue, your strong nose, your skin pale as northern light. So you see that of course I remember you, my dear, I remember you often. You must be timeworn now, your creases graceful and majestic, your prioress shoulders as sturdy as my mule-driving back. I can see you reading this, bundled up by your corner window in the refectory, near the fire, as when I was a little girl at your skirts, but attended now by your new novices; have a pintxo *with a cup of wine, have some peppers, Mother; fetch the breviary and hie yourselves to matins, daughters.*

One more cup, dear aunt, come drink with me and I shall tell you the rest. May this letter serve as a confession. As an act of contrition; though I am innocent, my crimes are many, so many that they will impart great suffering upon you, of this I am certain. Yet I trust as well that it will gladden your heart to have news of me, and to know that I have not forgotten you. And you must know that I repent ...

"Hey, che, your oranges, how are they?"

"They are about this big, Mitākuña. Thick skin. Made of wedges. Every wedge has little transparent sacks filled with delicious water. And some seeds."

"Mba'érepa?"

"Seeds because they are fruits, and fruits bear seeds. Wedges because that is what they have. Some fruits have wedges and others do not, just as some trees grow straight and others crooked. Do you understand, Michī?"

"You want to look for your oranges, che?"

"Well, that is a fine idea. We'll go soon. Let me write a little longer."

... I repent, aunt, I am changed. Of all my crimes, there is one, abandoning you, that you alone may forgive. Of the rest, perhaps the Lord Our God in his infinite mercy may grant me absolution. The jungle already has done so, I am sure of it. This letter will be long.

Memory deceives, and defies swiftness; it is miserly to one who flees, and relishes withholding from he who lies and changes his name, his people, his nation. I wonder how it is for you who have always lived on the selfsame ground, with the selfsame folk, the selfsame slow ceremonies one day after the next, and the selfsame trees that grow in the same unhurried way. Your memories, are they knotted to the boughs of the walnut tree we planted together? They must have grown, both memories and boughs, and fruits and leaves, slow and pretty as the rounded treetop toward the sky, and the trunk rooted who knows how far down, dear aunt ...

"Hey, che."

"No."

... and thus, slow and grave and fragile and strong as a tree must your hours remain, my dearest, more or less alike among themselves, as the walnuts born in springtime and harvested in the autumn; yet I know they are not completely equal; they each reveal small differences that must also be vertiginous and large, a storm on the open sea for those who live their lives attentive to the subtlest signs of constant cycles, the negligible infinity of identical shapes; perhaps all of life has been apportioned a share of vertigo and each life is

called to employ it in its own fashion. Or perhaps not, as indeed we are not dealt the same share of crimes. Oh, my hand trembles, beloved aunt, I have upset my inkwell in attempting to set down the first word in the long line of my offenses; they were not attributed to me, I committed them. Perhaps it will torment you to hear of me, and menace you with mortal troubles in your hours of prayer. You will pray for me, will you not? Do so: I beg of you, take pity on me.

The spirit of flight took hold inside my soul like the tiny roots in the walnuts you so lovingly gathered on Christmas Eve for later, for the Nativity, forty years ago, as you sought to soothe the tears I wept as a little girl, and so you did; I longed to return home, as you knew, for I had been parted at a tender age from my mother, from my little bay horse, from my brothers and their warlike games, from the embers of my kitchen hearth. None of this was mine, though I could not know such a thing at four years old. You sat me down in your lap, you dried my tears, you showed me a walnut, and you promised a tree to my bewildered eyes. You kept your promise.

"Che, señor."

"Antonio. Call me Antonio. Mitãkuña, please, be still."

… The next day, at the Christmas feast, you held three walnuts in your hand. One, perhaps all, would become a tree, you said. An entire tree was contained inside the nut, and all it needed was water and peace, and I would soon see. You cracked one end of the shell with a hammer. You tipped a few drops of water into the hole. You took a length of linen, wet it in the bowl, and wrapped it around the nut. You helped me do the same with the other two. We tucked them away in a corner of the storehouse. We collected earth from the pine grove of the convent. My small hands collected it, delighted, eager for saplings, for birth. I trembled, dear aunt, the day we returned and found that two of the nuts had sprouted; a *rattail, but white and sharp at the tip. That is what you told me then and still I remember. Amazed, I could only whisper, I felt that I could not speak aloud before the miracle of the walnut. Young as I was, I knew I had witnessed a sacred thing, the very burgeoning of life, constrained in a single point and splaying out into the infinite.*

As with the walnut, so it was for me; the man I am, contained in the girl I was, like the new tree clasped in the fruit of the old. So did the wish to escape and roam the world take root in me, a delicate root that thickened into stalk and stems and leaves and rounded canopy, just as my legs and hair did grow, and oh, my breasts. Innocent, my body; innocent the walnut and the tree of which the nut was born, and grew; and innocent the birds that live within it, alongside it, and the shadow under which you may still shelter on some summer afternoons, and which surely shelters the sheep, the pigs, the dairy cow, your custards. And the walnuts. Do you understand what I am saying? I think you must. I remember how you trembled, aunt, how your entire body quavered when you told me tales of men, because you told me also of God, of saints and angels and virgins, but your body quivered, and my little head felt it in your lap only when you spoke of men, men of the New World, of America, and their souls, likewise innocent, but damned nonetheless.

"Hey, che."

The girl speaks very quietly. Antonio ignores her and carries on. Writing to his aunt feels like being whisked on a sled down a gentle snowy slope, it fills him with sweet vertigo. He wants to stay there.

"Che, Antonio."

In that warm recollection. Having just one name, harboring no other secret than the itch to leave. To wander here and there, on ships, in wagons, walking or galloping. Encountering strange people and lands, vast seas, lofty mountains. Making friends. Conquering worlds for the glory of his king. Swimming with dolphins. Discovering treasure. Climbing trees. Eating luscious fruits. Waking at any hour he pleased. Not having to obey anyone, nor be punished, nor spend his days locked up inside, praying with his eyes fixed to the ground. The larger monkey shrieks. The dog barks. The horses scatter. He doesn't know where the quill he was clutching has fallen, a mere instant ago, as his daydreams drift.

"Hey, che."

He hears the rattle. A snake. He's lucky to have his sword within reach. A bit blunted but better than nothing. He stands, armed, and stamps the earth with his feet. He listens. Silence, save the growls of the dog slowly calming. The horses wander back. He wants to keep writing. He needs to leave the girls somewhere safe. The tree. He wraps them in his cape. Michī is so weak that he supports her head by pulling the cloth taut. He puts the monkeys in, too, binding them to his back, and climbs. He lays them down in a nest-like gathering of boughs and ties the cape to the strongest branch. He sits with them. An African once told him tales of enormous serpents. One had swallowed an elephant. It looked like a hat, said the man. His troops wouldn't need an enormous one to devour them. Any old serpent could gobble the girls and the monkeys for breakfast.

As long as he keeps writing, he feels that they're safe. As long as his body can hold up his head, his back, his hand, his eyes. He also fears. Even his eyelashes are heavy. He hears the mare. She snorts. Magnificent. Pure light, her muscles could be wrought of bronze, yet she's supple. A mount worthy of a venerable gentleman, a heroic warrior. And gentle too. Patiently she nurses her colt. And caresses him with her nose, licks him, guards his sleep. Would she nurse the girls? How long has he been writing? Are they still alive? He sets aside his quill. He climbs. Reaches them. Feels their breathing: weak but steady. They're at peace. They aren't hungry. He decides to stay for a while, up in the tree, by the nest. He's a big ugly bird without a song. He listens. The jungle's murmur is ceaseless. It's a single sound, but comprises thousands of voices. Each following its own particular melody. He understands that what he's hearing is also the jungle itself. What is it? A colossal conversation? Not just the multitude of trees and animals, but something immaterial they share. A relationship. Or many relationships. He thinks he'd be able to sense men approaching. The magpie would shrill, other birds would beat the air and shake the branches in their flight, others would go silent. He thinks they'll be safe if he listens. If he writes, as he promised his Virgin, and confesses, and repents, then they'll be safe. So he descends—slowly, slowly, he's exhausted—and sits down again, next to Red, who awaits him, and picks up the quill by the fire, under the palms. And he lets himself sink down into his childhood again. So far away.

4

Antonio saw them, he was watching them. Astonished. He couldn't understand how such skeletal forms had retained enough fat to send up smoke. Much less those Indians. He'd spent over twenty years in the New World and couldn't remember anything else like it. Still, not one of his cellmates turned their head to glance through the porthole.

"Seen the Indians?"

"What for. Always the same old story with them."

"Too stupid even to die as God wills."

"Shut up, eunuch, and let me sleep, or I'll hang you before the executioner can."

He's killed for less. Take the man in the tall hat who blocked his view of the comedy. The wretch who called him a cuckold when he won a hand at cards. The dolt who wanted to overtake him on a bend in the road and gave him a shove, baying that he was a villain. The Indian he dismembered for killing his second lieutenant in Araucanía. He could count many more men who'd met his knife, sword, or harquebus, but he left his memory in peace. Today he didn't care about the dead or about his honor either. So he kept quiet and lowered himself onto the heap of his chains, the ground a soupy mix of shit and spit and urine, overwhelmed by what he'd seen and even more so by what he began to think he hadn't. Nothing. On the eve of his execution, he wondered for the first time if he'd been blind for all these years. His body went cold. So dark and cold was the cell that he doubted he'd be capable of moving even if his chains should fall away. So too did he suspect that thus he'd perish: on the eve of his sentence. Distracted by the ladle knocking against the pot, he shifted as if he hadn't nearly died a moment prior. He was hungry. His body drove him to the door with such eagerness that the certainty of survival overpowered him; he looked like a new man when the soldiers finally appeared with the food and dished it hot into his hands. He missed cutlery, he wasn't an animal, but he didn't protest. It was roast meat: bonfires are a fine excuse for hours of grilling. The scent of the flesh consumed by tangling flames.

He sat on the ground, clutching a rib as long as a sword, grazed by a beam of languid reddish light that began to fade beside him, in the shit. He plunged his face into the meat and gnawed. He took the cup of wine that the bishop had asked the captain to grant the prisoners for the feast of the great fire on the Lord's day. The next course might be a lashing before he met the gallows. Unless the authorities had been mollified by the self-sacrificing soldiers, Christian martyrs on the pyre. Or by the wine. Or by the baptized Indian girls they'd be parading to their chambers, dragged off by the soldiers responsible for their lordships' intimate affairs. He peered through the bars. The sky a darkening orange, a blue turning bluer.

The sky stayed blue, pregnant with the shining orange of the Misiones jungle even at night. Grooved with great rivers. So near and so far from the Jesuits, from the Portuguese, from the ocean, from the ship that carried him away from Spain. It was a different world back there. And even more different tomorrow at the same hour. Barring a miracle, he was bound to look like this morning's hanged men look now. Strung from the noose like squash on the vine. No seeds but those the worms reduce them to. No fate conceivable but utter dark. Anguish clutched him. He wished with all his strength, prayed that there was nothing after death. If there were, he was certain that paradise wasn't within his grasp. The stone in his throat began to dissolve. Into water. He wept, Antonio, flooded with an emotion he couldn't understand. It was the music playing at the spit roast, he realized. The voices, made one when joined together, overwhelmed him. It was the Indian children. The voices belonged to the Indian children, the choir entering his body like a miracle. As if someone were shining a lantern on him in the darkest night. Or showing him the dazzling exit from the grave. The children of these jungles can sing as a nut would sing, if a nut could sing—and could it?—on germination. Sweet voices. The breath of God bathing the world in a peaceful golden light. He knew not only that he was alive, but that life was caressing him with the joy of pups, of flowers flowering, of pure love offered forth unthinking, of the birth of Christ. He thought he felt His soft, plump hand grasping his finger. Antonio softened, his dark eyes gleamed. He'd heard these Indian child choirs before. He could hear them now:

The Virgin pure went walking
from Egypt to Bethlehem
and halfway on the journey
the Child, he thirsted then.

"Don't ask for water, dear one,
don't ask for water sweet,
for the rivers trickle turbid
and the brooks are dank and bleak."

Now high up on the mountain
grew a weathered orange tree.
A blind man sat to guard it;
what would he give to see?

"Oh blind man, tell me, blind man,
would you an orange give
to soothe a thirsty child
and bring him some relief?"

"Oh lady, my dear lady!
Take all the fruit you need."
The Virgin, pure and righteous,
reached out to pluck just three.
The Child, only a child,
craved all that he could see.

After the Virgin parted,
the man no more was blind.
"Who was that righteous lady
who remedied my sight?"
It was the Holy Virgin
on her way to Bethlehem.

Blind. A blind man who began to see. He was being summoned: they were singing to him. It must have been the Holy Virgin, leading him out of the dark. Could the Holy Virgin, traveling from Egypt to Bethlehem, speak to the Indians? Dizzy, he thought hard. He recalled his life in the convent, the catechisms, the masses, the sermons of his aunt the prioress. He made his judgment: indeed, she could be the Holy Virgin. And why not? The Indians too had been baptized. They too were Catholic. They died like white men. The child who'd upset the wine had burned like all the others on the pyre. And the Virgin's love is greater than the world. Antonio sighed with relief. He didn't notice the vulture circling above, in the bluest blue, in the heights of the sky. It soared about, coasted on the air's hottest currents, above the tallest peaks. The vulture smelled Antonio's dinner and apprised, without envy, the crunch of his bite. It observed activity around the gallows. The soldiers left their posts to eat as well, and the dead relaxed and swayed in the breeze. This was what the vulture had been waiting for. So it shifted, almost imperceptibly, the two longest tips of its left wing. Slowly it descended, tightening its circles. The other vultures received the message—that there's a feast afoot—and started closing in from all sides. The discoverer alighted first atop the most corpulent hanged man, who shuddered on the noose, transformed into a fat, plumed angel, dark and purulent. An instant later, his comrades in death underwent the same transformation. The vultures, a gluttonous legion, shook the corpses as if putting out a fire. Antonio paid no heed. His night would have gone otherwise if he'd known that this could be his body's future: as food, tomorrow. For birds of prey.

Had he been blind? Had he just experienced a miracle, like the blind man of the orange grove? Why would the Virgin speak to him at all? He was neither virginal nor virtuous, he had lived in sin and killed multitudinously and never gifted any oranges to any thirsty children. Or maybe he had, why not. He couldn't remember having ever harmed a child. Well, no baptized child. You can never know for sure, in a world infested with Jesuits insistent on christening heathens right and left, in jungles and on mountains, in deserts and savannas, in rivers and seas. But he could've easily given his oranges to some child. Baptized or not. His mind drifted, borne aloft by the choir, and once again he was a little girl in the arms of his aunt. In the convent of Saint Mary of Donostia. Holy Mary. The Virgin. He needed to speak to someone. No one around him seemed to hope for anything except the chance to flee. Or death: they all already feigned rigor mortis. Yet he felt their vigilant breathing. Their broken prayers. Their eyeballs twitching under their lids. They were afraid, these prisoners. He wasn't, not anymore. He knew he would live. Why else would the Virgin open his eyes? He couldn't be certain. He could still die with the grace of a fleeting miracle. The convent. Over thirty years had passed since he'd left. In his ghastliest nightmares, he returned. He had never written to anyone. He promised the Virgin a long, endlessly long letter. He began to mumble it:

"I am as innocent and forged in the image and likeness of God as any other."

No, no. He faltered. Innocent, innocent he was not. But innocent of the crime that was about to lead him to the gallows—yes, that he was. So he kept going.

5

Mere days have passed, little more than hours, since he started pondering the letter to his aunt. But he's immersed in the tale, as if everything he's ever done has been for the specific purpose of telling her about it. He scarcely notices his own penmanship. A slow and laborious scrawling. He's almost forgotten his promise, he wants the letter to arrive. Wants his aunt to read it. Wants her to know this about him, to know this life that somehow became his own. He rests the quill in the ink, his back against the tree. He crushes a tiger ant before it bites him. Barely aware. Shuts his eyes in meditation. What he writes both is his life and isn't. It's not that he's lying. Though how couldn't he be. He's traveling through it once again. He chooses, of course, which parts of those days that were his to set down in the letter. Not all of it fits. And—this plunges him into perplexity—the account contains much of what hadn't fit there while it was still happening. Or something like that, none of this quite makes sense to him yet. He writes aloud to the prioress:

"How do we experience something that was there, but remained unseen? Is it part of our life? What we allow to pass us by as if it had not existed? What we glimpse today for the first time but which transpired some forty years ago; did we indeed live it at all? Is it true, what I'm telling you now?"

He stops. Hears whispers. His skin bristles like fur. He doesn't even think. He's already standing, sword in hand. Body seized by lightning. All the air inside. The girls! He glances up. They're still there. Mitākuña points a finger down. Their two small heads peek out. He releases the air he'd gathered as if he were about to leap into the river. The sword drops too. He climbs. The monkeys scale his shoulders all by themselves. Not the girls. He descends. Spreads the cape by the fire. Arranges all the creatures there. Asks them to be still. Mitākuña says yes. And keeps speaking. Saying what, Antonio doesn't know. Or to whom. Maybe it's a song. It is. A lullaby it seems. Mba'érepa? Mba'érepa? Michī joins the tune. A little drum. A rhythm. Antonio says he's going off in search of fruit and water. He ought to tie them up. If they escaped, even a toothless jaguar cub could eat them. The fire deepens their hollows, marking the volume of their little bones, the sunken grooves under their eyes, their ashen skin. They're not going anywhere. The monkeys leap, getting stronger. Into a tree that looks more like a bush, short and squat, croaking as with a thousand throats. Packed with toucans eating. The largest macaw drops a fruit to his feet. He tastes it. Sweet, acidic. Almost like a good orange. He picks some and doesn't care that the birds shit straight onto his head. It doesn't smell bad, toucan shit; it has a metallic, blue-black gleam. The ballrooms will have to wait. For now, food. He chews a bit for Michī. Will the mare want to nurse them? Mitākuña says that the fruits are called ubajay and she doesn't like them. But she eats anyway, the corners of her lips tugging toward her neck. At once he feels their rhythmic breathing. All is calm. He eats some fruit himself. Red curls up between his knees. And he picks up the quill.

You told me of the Admiral, my aunt, of how Christopher Columbus had sailed from Sanlúcar, of caravels like walnut shells, of how he'd wished to travel to one place but found himself in quite another, and founded a world there, of the Indians who sailed on rafts cut from the bases of trees, marvelously carved, you said. In your cell you told me of that other world, and you filled it with lords, with ships, with Indians, with strange lands, though all lands were strange to me save those of the convent, as they were to you, my dear. I was your little girl and you let your mind roam and led me into your American daydreams, with all those souls awaiting conversion to the one true faith, and in that moment I had no knowledge of it, but the thirst for world was growing in me, the thirst to leave that place, to meet those innocent people who gifted skeins of spun cotton and parrots to the admiral. Oh, parrots, a thing of beauty, if you could see them you would also see that the colors here are alive, made of flesh and feather, humming blues, shrilling reds, yellows, greens. And they also brought spears to Columbus, who gave them glass beads and bells in return, watching meanwhile for gold, and he saw that some wore a bit of it strung from a hole in their nose, and communicating with gestures he came to learn that in the South was a king with great cups of it. He embarked in search of gold, and said—our Portuguese, our Jewish, our Italian admiral of the Spanish imperial armada—that the island was very large and very flat and very green with trees and wet with many waters and an enormous lake in the middle, all without a single mountain, all green, a delight to look upon, and its inhabitants meek. The girl I was heard your words and begged you to repeat them until I learned them by heart, so I could remember them as needed, and I lost myself in ships, saw myself sailing away, my hair streaming like gentle waves, spreading over your prioress skirts, yearning for seas, becoming sea myself with sheer desire to melt into the cracks of the convent floors and go where water forever goes, which is toward water, have you noticed that water is apportioned into parts that are sometimes vast and sometimes very small, but that they always like to gather together?

"Hey, che."
"What?"

"Tell me about the lady."

"What lady, Mitākuña?"

"The one called Virgin, che."

"She is the mother of the Lord Our God."

"Who is God? And his papa?"

"The papa of God is God."

"And the mama is the Lady, Yvypo Amboae?"

"Mba'érepa?"

"Because she carried him in her womb and then gave birth to him. As mothers do."

"Mba'érepa?"

"Because God chose her, Michī."

"Who is God, che?"

"He who created the heavens and the earth."

"No."

"Yes."

"And he had a mitā with his same name, che?"

"What is a mitā?"

"You know nothing, che. A baby."

"Yes. No. The baby is Himself but incarnate."

"I do not understand."

"Mitākuña, time for sleep."

… Have you noticed that water is apportioned into parts that are sometimes vast and sometimes very small, but that the parts always like to gather together?

Water wants water and my soul longed to wander, dear aunt, and that is how I imagined a life lived far from the convent, far from the mournful discipline of dawns on my knees, of the endless, funereal lists of sins, and the brief lists of virtues for a woman, briefer for novices and briefer still for professed nuns; to obey and desire Jesus Christ alone. I did not profess, as well you know. Forgive me, aunt.

I had an epiphany, a revelation, I felt the call and could not resist it, for no one can, my dear. I would not be a prisoner of the convent, or of anything else. I left. I had yearned to be a sailor but never, never, never did I know that such a thing could be, and the will for what cannot be ends up paining the flesh, and this pain was fierce; I felt it in my bones, in my muscles stiff from confinement, in the eyes I was obliged to lower, in my hands, bound as they had been. The pain kept me still and quiet until your keys pressed themselves on my eyes and heart and entire body, as the ground presses itself on what falls, and I felt my own little root snap inside, and I did not doubt, could not doubt, I knew of neither good nor evil, I did not ask myself if it was a sin, an affront against the Lord My God, against your good love, against my own soul; if I would later burn not merely in Hell but also in the bonfires of the Holy Inquisition. My body glimpsed the door and departed like the shoot of the walnut through the damp notch we made there. I spent three days and three nights in our Donostian woods, next to the convent you ruled almost with innocence—for our family ruled; does it still?—you must still rule with the ease of a cause on an effect. My family was a cause and I knew I would be no prisoner, just as you knew your lot and never doubted it, just as those in power do; just as it is known that thunder follows lightning. Such knowledge is given to the triumphant: the king and the Pope know and governors know, too. The others doubt their various doubts. Malleable on occasions and on others like an iron shackle.

Those who flee also know as if they ruled, because they rule themselves; if they doubted, they would not flee. Have you seen that those who leave because they simply yearn to leave are certain as well? The sureness of a compass, whose north is nothing but its distance from wherever it began, that's how it is, and was. And will be. And so forth every time since then. I knew I would be no prisoner, I would sooner be a hunter, and I returned to the world I nonetheless did not know; I was summoned by the air of the woods, the horses whose hooves I once heard clopping from inside the convent, the voices of the outside, the metallic clanging of swords, the heavy footfall of men. Your sweet voice telling me tales of another world. The strength of my legs driving me to walk. Yet I had been afraid for years. Until you, my aunt, my family, everything I loved, sent me to fetch your breviary for matins, and I glimpsed the great key, long as my hand and forearm, like a knife, dark and ferrous and heavy, forged for the ruthless doors of our convent, and I felt as if it had opened me, as if my own doors—and I was a cold, secluded cell—had been flung open, and the sun had shone in, and who would ever close such doors and confine themselves to the dark again?

I did not hesitate; I seized a needle and thread, seized some shears, seized four lengths of cloth, and oh, eleven coins, because the apostles were twelve, but no one wants a traitor in their midst. I left forever. I was afraid, it was the dead of night, I could not remember having ever tread any ground but the gray stones and leafy earth of the convent gardens; yet my legs were not afraid and led me forth. Neither were my hands afraid, my dear, they took what could be taken, and opened what must be opened for me to go, and my body ran to the woods like a fawn when the eyes of the tiger rest, at last, on the hide of another beast, or on the flight of an insect, or on the river. And no, I knew nigh nothing of anything, I was innocent as a caged beast; if the cage opens it emerges, aunt, and what is there to know.

"Hey, che, tell us who is God. How did he make sky and earth?"

"I will tell you, Mitākuña, if you promise to sleep when I have finished."

"All right."

"Nahániri."

"Promise me or nothing, Michī."

"I promise for her. She sleeps no matter what, che. Sing to us, you, sing us that song."

"Very well, I will sing. It goes like this."

> *In the beginning God*
> *Made all the earth and heavens.*
> *But they were mixed together,*
> *A gaping chasm covered*
> *Entirely with darkness.*
> *And there was also water.*
> *The spirit of this God*
> *Flew over from the East.*
> *Yet he saw nothing there.*
> *Let there be light, he said:*
> *Now fiat lux! Fiat lux!*
> *Fiat lux! Now fiat lux!*
> *With his creating word—*

"Nahániri."
  "Tell her to be still or no more singing."
  "Ekirirī, Michī, che."

> *With his creating word*
> *Now there was light and God*
> *Could see that it was good.*
> *And so he called it Day*
> *And called the darkness Night.*
> *And so the first day went.*
> *Now fiat lux! Fiat lux!*
> *Fiat lux! Now fiat lux!*

"Nde japu is what you say. Lies."
  "You must sleep. Go to sleep, Mitākuña."
  "Tell the truth, che."

"What truth?"

"Your God, what did he eat?"

"Nothing. God needs nothing. He is not hungry. Or sleepy. He is never tired."

"Mba'érepa?"

"Nde japu, che."

"It's not a lie. I will tell you what God ate if you promise to sleep."

"What foods did he eat?"

"He ate clouds. And from his mouth he spat out the light. And with his farts, the darkness."

"Heeheehee. Nde japu, che."

"I swear it is the truth, Mitãkuña. Now sleep. Look, I will show you more of the darkness."

He lets out a colossal fart. The girls cover their noses with their hands and uncover them, shrieking with laughter. The monkeys dart into the trees. The horses snort. Red, satisfied with her portion of jerky, doesn't even stir. They reconvene. The monkeys return with fruits that look like artichokes. With a sweet taste somewhere between pineapple and banana.

"Hey, che, these are your oranges?"

"You know they are not."

"And where are your oranges?"

"In Spain."

"Chirimoyas, these."

"Very well."

The insects hush their drone. Each and every animal living in the green tapestry of the boundless jungle and the trees and the vines and the flowers and the mushrooms and the mosses too go quiet. The tatiná, the cloud that rises up from the river to crown the trees and dampen everything, halts as well. It's the time of day when all is peace. When even the tides conclude and nothing kills or dies. Except for the new men, but even they sometimes forget their own novelty. And they sigh, their gazes lingering on something unknown to them.

6

He couldn't die this way. In mortal sin. It would be a double death, definitively dead is what he'd be, or worse, burning in the lakes of Hell. He's tarnished the temple of his body and the name of the Holy Mother Church. He needs a priest. Any priest. The poorest, dimmest, most malignant old priest —even his worst enemy. Surely an Indian priest would do. Or even a Jewish priest. Truly anything to offer absolution and let him go in peace, if go he must. Death was catching him unconfessed. Still as stone, in his chamber lined with purple velvet, the hall with a bedroom whose construction he'd commanded, adjacent to the church. He'd had the tapestries shipped in from the Motherland. A noble prelate's dignity couldn't be abandoned to the fates of the New World. Yet there he was. His white belly spilling onto the eminently regal burgundy carpet. His baby-angel curls crushed against his skull; his watery eyeballs stitched with red and surging from their sockets; red-faced, his neck veins swollen as trunks and plowed with bubbles that swelled into globes until they broke loose and streamed forth like liquid. Soon they bumped into some new obstacle and ballooned again. His blood careening crazily as musket fire. And the air that couldn't enter. And the voice that couldn't leave. He opened his entire mouth, exposing his glottis: the bishop was missing his molars. He wanted to speak. He needed to call for help. Needed someone to rush to his aid. Needed to confess. Of his body he felt only the lacerating pain that cut off his breath, the hurled spear in his chest that pinned down his voice and everything else. He also felt his cock throb beneath his cassock. And managed to pray for God to forbid it:

"Fiat voluntas tua, but please do not allow it, Father, my Lord, do not allow my seed to spill onto the earth, Father, do not forsake me."

He prayed. And beheld the scene before him in the early morning light, barely veiled by the fine purple drape over his enormous window. Little more than shadows, but he knew the fortress's morning routines. The disfigured silhouettes of the Indian women. Broken dolls, marionettes drawn and impaled like girl Christs. It was only drunken soldiers fornicating with maids. But how sinister the shadows. Two-headed, four-legged monsters shuddering in their horrid throes. He was surprised he could be surprised, mortally winded as he was. And the soldiers snoring on the ground or crooning with the vaporous bliss of the voided body. He tried to swallow air. And it wouldn't come. And it wouldn't go. But no one noticed because no one was supposed to know that he was watching. It was his secret. And the men respected him for it, pretending they had no idea. There was no window in the wall of his chambers. They didn't hear the lashes he dealt himself in punishment for his own urge to sin. Or the vulture caws he emitted when he spilled his seed in vain. His men understood that this behavior was among the ways of holiness. The bishop didn't touch women or touch himself, except with the whip. The prelate watched them but they didn't see him, and in the end they forgot. Like now, forgotten by his sheep, by God, and worst of all, by air. The air that wouldn't enter him. It entered Mitãkuña instead. She released it slowly from her mouth. Revealing the tiny serrations of her brand-new teeth. She opened her tapered eyes, moving. The bishop was watching her. He wanted to reach out his hand. Plead for her aid. Tell her to run for a priest. Any priest. He couldn't die this way. But neither could he speak. The girl, terrified, understood. The door of her cage was open. The others were shut. She couldn't open them by herself. Too weak. She had to walk. Slip off without a moment's hesitation and go for help. She knew it, and so did the little red dog who whimpered from the shadows and then emerged and followed her. They walked. Grazing against each other in the bubble they made together. Almost floating, their feet barely touching the ground. Nearly invisible, so small were their shadows. They fit in the shadow of everything else. They needed to seize this moment in which all was suspended if they were to elude the soldiers' grasp. The bishop prayed.

"Sed libera nos a malo."

He tried to breathe again. The air wouldn't come out, but some tears did, he wept like a wineskin ready to burst, and burst he did. His mouth exhaled its final, fetid air, and his seed and all else capable of flowing then flowed between his belly and the burgundy rug. His mouth and eyes stayed open. What wretched luck: he could indeed die in sin and without a priest to offer absolution. In what moment of that passage between life and death is a man responsible for his own licentiousness? If such is the word for a dying man's swollen cock. Death hadn't swelled it. Those Indian whores were to blame. And the soldiers, fornicating willy-nilly like pointy springs. What a long minute, the minute of the bishop's death.

Now he's prey to the flies. One alights on him, intrepid. There are no consequences. It summons the others, and they start to lay their eggs inside the cavities of the illustrious prelate, who undergoes an extraordinary metamorphosis into the larvae's roost.

7

He cuts and works a branch. Sullenly. He whets it sharp. Antonio pares off shaving after shaving as a soft and undulating light seeps through the mist and foliage. The tip, sharper and sharper. He wants it fit to pierce a fat fish with a single blow. He slices through a fern with a single graze. There it is. A marvel of a sword: he's barely honed it. And now he's forged a spear just as strong and razor-edged. He's seen Indians fish with spears. He slashed a path to the river, but how can this be: it's overgrown again. He opens it back up. He's tired. He wants to eat. And sleep. He shouldn't sleep. He stands, sunk into the riverbank that sucks at him, how foul, how crude this new world with its clay lips. He coats himself in mud to trick the fish. The sun rises. The clay cracks. Insects ring him like clouds around a mountain peak. The caimans form a circle a few paces off. He stays still, still. Until a dorado nears. Enormous, it must be nearly a meter long, he could smoke it and they'd eat for ten days. He holds his breath and flings his spear, which splits and vanishes, cleaved in two, with the current. He strikes the fish. Stunned, it hesitates. Not Antonio. He lunges. Once, twice, three times. The fish eludes him deftly in swift diagonal swerves. Until it sinks to a certain depth. Antonio too. He weeps and bathes himself. Dresses. He'll need to hunt, and with his sword: he can't make any noise or the captain will discover them. Or he'll have to convince the mare to nurse the girls, and he'll go another day on fruit alone. Better convince the mare. And he sets to work on a trap. He retraces the new path he cut. The brush is denser than it was four hours ago. He's distracted. A scent. Lovely. Of food. Silently he approaches the camp. Delicious. He runs. Indian food. Red terracotta bowls, bright and steaming. They must be close. There doesn't seem to be a soul around. He deliberates between hunger and prudence. He considers waiting for the girls to eat before he does. Hunger wins and they eat together. When they're finished, Michī falls asleep at once. Not Mitākuña. She leans back against the palo santo tree, beyond the shelter of the palms, and sketches in the earth with a stick. Antonio lies down on the cape to rest. He asks Mitākuña to tell him if anything strange happens. He doesn't know what strange might mean to her.

"If the tiger comes, or the snakes. If the Spaniards come, the ones who look like me."

She says yes and stays seated there. Antonio doesn't want to fall asleep. He wakes past noon. Red slumbers in his lap. Mitākuña on her watch. Contented, he thinks of what belongs to him. His life. What didn't matter. What he didn't notice. What he barely understood. And all of that, he's astonished to think, is what led him to where he is now. Just as he was led by what he did see. How to understand it. How to explain. He forgets about the trap he'd resolved to set. And he writes:

I ran, dear aunt. I felt the ocean like the breath of an enormous animal spurring me onward, how had I failed to feel it before, it lent me strength and caressed me with its colossal teeth, if such a thing could caress, if such vastness could have teeth. It was a beast as great as the sky, the open cross-country sky one sees outdoors, which grew with every step, and blued all things, even the rumbling of the sea, and freedom rose before me like an apparition, with a spectral light, as from beyond the grave, and thus did I first encounter the light of the open elements; the stars gleamed like signals, shone white and red, they twinkled, spilled restless with the moonlight onto the earth, trembling together, casting brilliant shadows, how could it be? That's what I remember. They taught me possible directions, they spoke to me; not that way, Catalina, but this way, take this path and that one, and in my empty head and my entire body the stars resounded, their glimmers splintered in me, and the ocean made me into its song of wind and called my name, but its shores harbored my father's ships, and my legs marched toward the scent of the forest, which was mint and earth wet with dew, for the earth opens at night and lets out its breath, a damp breath full of secret life, of roots, of worms, of dead creatures, and of seeds splitting softly into life. The woods called to me as only the cooking pot of Sister Josefa had called to me until then, or your tales; the forest called to me as a home would call, but a home filled with strangers because the forest is also made of many animals, though not so many as the jungle; it is, the forest, a beast of winter, though it blooms in spring; have you noticed, aunt, that the forest is an animal? Do you let yourself be comforted by its breath? Our Donostian forest is made of animal eyes that spy with fear, with ferocity, and perhaps with hunger, and, I must tell you now, with forgiveness as well. The trees protect, are always protecting, and thus I fled the convent and fled the roaring of the sea and fled my own thick mane that tugged me back, I fled to the water, the water, to the ships, Catalina, but my father was on the ships, or to your skirts to hear tales of sailors as you combed my locks, but my father was there too. I climbed a tree and cut my hair. And I left you. And I left my hair scattered across the dead leaves. There it remains, I am sure of it, buried under mushrooms and worms.

"Hey, che, Antonio."

"…"

"Che, I am talking to you."

"I'm shocked, Mitãkuña. What is it?"

"What happened next?"

"Next after what?"

"After your god spat light and farted dark."

"Mba'érepa?"

"Because He farts, Michī."

The girls have just enough strength to laugh. Their cheeks flush. Antonio cackles too. Is this blasphemy? He isn't sure. He's committed worse. He's going to tell them the whole of Creation. He'll have to make up the song of the second day, and fast. Or maybe the entire week all together, if he can manage it.

And on the second day
God undertook the water
Vast as a great big sea,
No over and no under.
He said, Let there be vault
And let the waters sunder.
Fine work, said God. I think
It shall be called the Sky,
And rested for the day.
And then the third one dawned.
He dried a part of it
Then gathered up the water
And He named one the Earth
And dubbed the other Seas.
And on the Earth he called
For woods and wilds to grow.
They grew and they were good.

"Mba'érepa?"

"Because God wished it so. Let me go on, Michī."

"Che, be quiet, let him sing."

And so the next day God
Made stars, the sun and moon.
And then he stocked this world
With beasts like whales and fishes
And blackbirds and with chickens.
Now multiply, he told them,
And fill the seas and skies.
And they obeyed his wishes.
And all was merriment,
Praise be to God, hurrah!
The next day God created
The animals that walk
And crawl, climb, eat, and sleep.
He saw that they were good.
He told them, multiply.
And they began, obedient,
To carry out this task.
And all was merriment,
Praise be to God, hurrah!
And with his work near done
The Lord felt all alone,
And thus created man
Exactly in his image.
He made them male and female,
Female and male he made.
And all was merriment.
Praise be to God, hurrah!

"Hey, che, Antonio, is kuimba'e ha kuña your god?"
"What is that, Mitãkuña?"
"Man and woman. Like you, che."
"Well, I hadn't thought of it. I am a man."

"Héê. But you have one breast."

"Many men do."

"Mba'érepa?"

"Because they do, Michī."

"My papa and my grandpa and my uncles do not have one."

"Well, God and I do."

"Just one, che?"

"Mba'érepa?"

"Because, Michī. Let us sing together."

And all was merriment, praise be to God, hurrah! softly he sings to them. And at last they leave him in peace.

… You gave me a good life, dear aunt, and loved me well, but in confinement. You always said, "You are my little daughter, my first-born girl, my only neska, *and the abbey shall be your inheritance in my old age." But that was not my wish, I parted and I must have parted you in two, and it was for you that I wept in those first hours of solitude in the forest. Quietly I wept, awake, with the needle in my hand and the shears in my skirt, under the luscious inclemency of the dew that revived all things it touched and endowed them with silver glimmers, but chilled me to the marrow, beneath the gaze of a family of owls as meek as I myself, crouched and open-eyed, and my head turning in all directions, because dry leaves cover and conceal but also crunch and betray, and I remained the girl I was, for the man I am now was still in the making, I left myself stitch by stitch; from my shift I made a shirt, from my habit breeches and a doublet. The ruffled collar, dear aunt, was a request I had made of my father long before, as a game, on one of his rare visits to the convent, and he was unable to refuse. We did not know it then, nor he nor I, but that ruffled collar would be my sole bequest. Three days it took for me to finish the garments my legs entreated, my arms demanded. I felt newly strong as soon as the new suit slipped over my head. My*

entire body stretched, beloved aunt, my muscles forging themselves,
and I was free. The world felt within my grasp.

"If you take away my letter, I will—"

But no, they won't understand. The monkeys make their slow escape. They've recovered much of their strength but not yet their speed. He yells to them twice, retrieves his letter, and strokes the dog. And settles in to keep writing. Another mark on the paper. The dog paws at him cheerfully. No matter. He'll have to stop and scratch her head.

"And you lot?"

The mare and the colt are going about their business. They nibble flowers, ferns, wander about a bit, straying further each time, and return to their spot beside the cape. Tall and gold as suns the both of them. Red curls up at his side. At last she stops pawing at his legs, demanding his attention. Now he can go on.

8

Ay, madre mía. Mama, mama, mama. O our Father. O my mother. Tremors quaked the bodies and uncorked their torrents, crazed and vertical as mountain rivers. First asleep, then awake. First guilty, then innocent. First young, then old. First the vulgar, then the noble. Now all at once. They wept. They wept so bitterly that they no longer knew quite who they were. Silently they wept. They lost their names and their ranks and their traits and their features, as if life itself were fleeing with their tears. The large of nose had their noses eroded. The puffy-mouthed had their lips whittled down to nothing. The pink-faced, the dun-faced, and the beige-faced went practically translucent as ghosts. All eyes swelled huge. They wept. As if expecting to wake shriveled into mummies and to revoke, by sheer dint of weeping, their executioner's ability to kill them. They wept. Not wanting to weep, weeping even without distress, some wept almost cheerfully, mindless on the eve of the gallows. And some wept with wrath. It didn't matter: however they wept, they expelled the same torrential tears.

Antonio—a four-stalked yrupé flower, one stalk per chain—didn't weep. He floated in the lukewarm current of his companions' weeping. Floating, he heard the sea, beheld the green peaks of Europe. Green as green wheat, green as the green lime. He was four years old, he didn't yet know how to read or write; he knew he didn't know and he didn't care. He hopped about, he danced, he was a girl, and her little white dress trembled like one of the tiny blossoms springing up in the grasses she tread. Sprinkled with petals like the lilies there, the lilies of his childhood, which were singing open-mouthed in the undergrowth. They had—she and the small mouths of the lilies that sang with her—a sweet, reedy voice like the voice of the Indian children's choir that had sung him the song about the Virgin pure, walking from Egypt to Bethlehem. The voice of all things holy. The voice of birds when they learn to fly. The voice of sperm whales when they graze the sky with a single leap, and plunge back into the sea, shattering it. The voice of baby elephants retreating to the shelter of their mothers' feet. The voice of the first stars after a storm. The voice of the open door, the flight from the cage. As they sang *Atharratz jauregian bi zitroiñ doratü* the sun caressed both girl and blooms. She danced toward the lambs, who bleated their tender counterpoint. She laced her fingers through her curls and sang louder *Huntü direnian batto ükhenen dü*. The little milk cow scampered over to meet her, followed by the calf, and she sang to them *Ahizpa, zuza orai Salako leihora* and they danced with the silly prancing of heavy beasts. Antonio danced in his sleep. Floating like a rowboat in the warm tears of the prisoners who rocked him like loving waters. As if he himself were a bee bathed in the singing crown of an ancient chestnut on the convent grounds. Bells clanged. The sun climbed. The vulture felt a pang of hunger as it roamed the jungle's silver-green dome with its eyes. Below, by the dungeon where Antonio was singing, the barracks' vast and gloomy square. The captain bellowed and the soldiers rushed to tackle the futile tasks, which, they hoped, would make them invisible to the fury of their commanding officer.

The captain had lost his friend the bishop and realized, horrified, that he had loved him. He also missed Fernández. Most of him largely strewn about by wind, Fernández was infusing a peculiar scent into the nectar of the long fuchsia flowers brightening a silk floss tree. And he clung to the bodies of bored wasps embarking in search of other blossoms. And he flew, Fernández: he flew and became the stuff of hives and found himself ensnared in a spider's web. The captain noted, moreover, the absence of the young priestlets who'd left to offer mass in the Indian villages. There was no one to inform him of the protocol for priests who die abruptly. And not just any death. The dignified dignitary, who would have known exactly what to do, was lying there mute, mouth agape, guzzling flies. Or, rather, the flies were guzzling him. Newborn larvae were digging networks of tunnels into his insentient body. The captain general wondered what sort of ceremony would befit such a preeminent authority of the Church. He didn't know. He didn't have time to read the regulations. He disliked the regulations. And given the choice between sitting down to invest the requisite time and attention or pounding the fingers of his right hand with a mallet, he'd choose the latter. Besides, what time. In this filthy jungle, bodies rot in the time it takes a cock to crow; several had crowed already. The fuming captain tromped his way through the square between the body of his friend—limbs stiff, torso swollen—and his office. He stopped short, pierced by the dulcet ray of a celestial voice singing in Biscayne. A little girl's voice. A voice like the voices of his sisters so long ago. A voice like the voice the little girl he'd left behind in Spain must sing with now. Soft and perfumed so sweetly that he struggled to lift his nose from her golden downy head. He felt that his daughter was singing to him, asking him to come home, and he thought perhaps he should. He'd already amassed a handsome hoard of gold. What else was there, if all he wanted now was to resuscitate the bishop, to share once more their little chats after supper, when they were nearly drunk, when it was almost time to sing lullabies in Biscayne. He could go home for that. Speak in his language all day long with everyone around him, and sing with his daughter and sniff the perfume that made him want to enfold her in his arms and shield her from all the ills of the world. Could this be some early proof of the dubious holiness of his friend the high prelate, who was sending signs of his better life in the beyond? He needed to find the impossible child. However impossible she may be, she was singing. He decided that the most prudent course of action would be to hurry off and express his gratitude to the Lord. To pray, while searching for the girl: not a moment to lose. The voice led him to the dungeons. He wondered if an angel had taken mercy on the filthy prisoners in his charge. That deposit of criminal flesh he'd stockpiled in the cells without knowing exactly what they'd done. Or why. Evidently, it would be wise, even magnanimous, to hang them as soon as their sentence was pronounced. Once he had a secretary again, and a bishop, he'd enlist their help in seeking the lawful, Catholic means to deal out a swifter form of justice for his convicts. He covered his mouth and nose against the stench of the humanity amassed there. He peered between the bars. And found his girl. She turned out to be a ghastly man, floating in a lake of excrement and tears. A man with a hooked nose and sturdy back, a martial mien, clawlike hands, burly arms, twisted lips and cheeks furrowed by the scars of endless duels. A man who all but danced as his thin lips released a

Atharratzeko zeñiak berak arrapikatzen;
Hanko jente gazteriak beltzez beztitzen.

It was the very same song his nursemaid sang when he, the captain general, was still a boy and wanted nothing more than to eat custard, play with his brothers, and cling to his mother's skirts, should he be fortunate enough to see her. He didn't care if it was the work of God or the Devil himself. He ordered the prison doors to be opened, confronting the odious stench for a good look at the convict girl. Antonio descended from the peak of the crest to the edge of the surf. The moisture of the inmates' weeping had loosened the nails that cleaved his chains to the walls. He rapidly emerged, conveyed by the little ocean that had kept him warm, bobbing and singing away his final hours. He woke, cheered, as the sun that scraped the red earth began to dry him. He was unruffled by the captain's face over his, nearly breathing his breath.

"Good morning, your lordship. May your day be fine, my captain, and God bless you."

"Do you not hear the clamor of the bells, prisoner? You have a most vigorous voice."

"Thank you, my lord: I am a baritone. Pray forgive me, my lordship, but I was dreaming of my homeland, my beloved Donostia, and all I could hear was the rumble of the sea and the lilies in song."

"Donostia, you say? I heard you singing in Biscayne with the voice of a girl. Can you read, prisoner?"

"Ego legere et scribere scio, mi domine, gratias agere Deo."

"And can you do sums, pray tell? Tell me, how many are three thousand five hundred forty-one plus one hundred eighty-two."

"Three thousand seven hundred twenty-three, your lordship."

The captain was delighted. He'd found his secretary. And he wouldn't rule out the possibility of installing the prisoner in his personal chambers, so he could hear these songs in his dreams. He commanded him to arrange the bishop's funeral rites and departed for his nap, relieved and humming, placid at last, now that his little girl was safe and sound.

9

The blow jolts him awake. The quill drops when his hand leaps to his brow. There's blood on his fingers and a projectile in his lap: a pod of the sort some call black man's ears. The foliage is still, as if made of nothing but leaves and branches. What isn't still, down below, where he left them, are the monkeys. Have they retreated to their own country by now? Two, three, ten more ear pods strike him as they fall. Furious, he stands and lobs them back into the canopy. Now some thirty more come tumbling down. He whirls a heavy bough toward the top of the trunk and it comes crashing back, right onto his head.

"Come down from there, you wretched monkeys!"

They come down. And leap back up again. And careen in circles around themselves, and around everything else in sight. And leap once more. And cling to the girls. They've brought some small yellow fruits. The monkeys nibble and share. The flesh is golden, slightly acrid, very sweet.

"This fruit is delicious. Bring us some more."

"Are they the oranges of your lady, che?"

"You know quite well that they are not, Mitākuña. More fruit, you imps."

They obey. A dozen pummel him from all directions. The girls' little cackles spur him on. Antonio sits, plucks the fruits from his body, from his clothes, and doles them out. Michī grabs the end of his captain's cape, now dusty red, the color of the earth itself, and dips it into the bowl of water, pressing it to his wound. And strokes his forehead with her feeble, clumsy, sticky hands. Antonio feels a lump in his throat. For an instant, he touches the top of Michī's head as if combing her hair. He walks over to the horses, which are nibbling orchids. The mare strains her sinewy neck to reach the white and purple flowers. Her golden snout against the moss. The violet labella plucked by the beast's sweet mouth. The colt prodding his hoof and nostrils against a fallen blossom before he licks it. Antonio picks a cluster of purple flowers. He offers it to the mare. Strokes her flank. Unsaddles her. Removes her bit. He croons that she too is a flower. She returns his sweetness with a few soft nuzzles, rests her head on his shoulder. He kneels, touches her udders. She lets him. He milks her a bit. Fills two bowls, no more—the colt must eat, too. Brings them to the girls. They don't want it. He sips a little. It's vile. But they need it. Where have there ever been babes who don't drink milk? Here? Do children drink milk in the New World? He doesn't know. They do in Spain. He remembers the tender convent cow, her pink udders, her calf. His aunt insisting he drain his cup each morning. Does Indian food have milk in it? Evidently they know how to feed their little ones. Or not. If they knew anything, they wouldn't be slaves, he thinks. Although, he reconsiders, one can know and lose regardless. Anyone can be a slave. Except for the king. He tries again. They won't open their mouths. He proposes a trade. A coin. Michī takes it. She passes it to Mitākuña. They stare at it together. Bite it. They don't like it. They toss it to the ground. They must be dim. He offers them the mare's carved bit. They're not interested. He offers them gold threads. Nothing. He despairs. In his desperation, he looks down and spots some spherical seeds. He makes various markings on them. Stripes here and there, parallel lines, crosses. Now he has their attention. He digs a small hole in the red earth. He draws a line a yard away. Tosses one of the tiny balls. Then another. They want to play. Only if they drink the milk, he says. They drink it. The dog and the monkeys watch with shining eyes. They play. They get all of the balls into the hole with just two throws each. Red pounces on a seed. She bites it. Darts about. The monkeys seize the other two. They clamber swiftly to and fro. They're recovering. The game delights them all. Antonio less so. He didn't even have to let them win. He doesn't think it's right, losing to two small girls who can't even speak properly in the Christian tongue and are malnourished to the point of simplemindedness. He doesn't like losing, no matter the tongue of his opponents. But he wants to return to his own affairs, and in this sense, he reassesses, he's won. They've all won. He didn't know such a thing was possible. The girls fall asleep again. Antonio gets back to his writing, with the lump in his throat still aching. Red sits in his lap.

So transpired my first escape, dear aunt, the desertion of my girlhood cell, the little window crosshatched by the green needles of pine, the diminutive violet flowers, the mushrooms that tasted of wood, fed on rain and cold and light from clouds so ponderous they threatened to fall from the sky, as if forged of fogged, dirty silver. I would be no prisoner. Rather a hunter, out of doors, in the world, when I believed that life was a dyad, and when I didn't know, could not grasp the trinity I know now. No prisoner. No hunter. I ponder. And doubt. No longer do I flee nor govern, even if I govern my own self, if govern my self I do at all.

"Hey, che, give me water."

"Have some water, little one."

"Pee. Take me, che."

They get up, walk some fifty steps among the palms. Antonio turns away. He hears when she's done.

"Time for sleep, Mitākuña."

She doesn't protest. Holds his hand on the way back. Falls asleep as soon as her head touches the cape. Antonio returns to his letter, despite the mosquitoes and his sweat. They're constant. He's getting used to them. Besides, he's shirtless. His torso looks like a field after a battle. There are pits. Heaps of rubble. Remnants of fire. Yawning ditches. Parts patched discordantly to other parts. And parts sundered with less concord still. Remnants of a minimal breast. The other side, just a scrap of skin.

"No longer do I flee nor govern, even if I govern my own self, if govern my self I do at all."

I know I wish to tell you of these things, of how I was first a prisoner and then a hunter as I traversed the world, walking and riding horseback and rowing or hoisting sails or astride a mule, and I came to know a freedom that I was, had always been, will always be?—denied. I have it, it belongs to me, and so I live on. It cannot be forbidden. Nonetheless, I doubt, I govern therefore I doubt. Is it truly mine? Can I possess what I have been forbidden? Could what I am be withheld from me? I did not wonder so on that first night in the forests my legs led me to, seeking shelter from the gazes of men who would not, in their turn, wonder what a maid could possibly be doing there, alone in the dark, in the veil of a novice. The epiphany of my escape was twofold; I knew I would need to dress as a man wherever I wished to roam. My legs impelled me so. My hair shirt impelled me so; I must free myself from it, so it was revealed to me, or I would die of gangrene, rotting and in pain. The convent walls impelled me so. As did your stories and the stitching I learned from you, as did our hardy shoulders. Will you fathom such a paradox? I have obeyed you always while never doing what you would have wished. Or else I have done what you wished without ever obeying. I learned this not long ago, here, in my jungle, with my animals, close to these people who are hardly as gentle as those of Columbus.

A scribble. He has just scribbled on his letter. It's the largest monkey's fault: it leapt onto his head. Slipped its hand into his pocket. Swung from a branch. Now swings from another. Up in the silk floss tree. Antonio suppresses his rage. He doesn't want to wake the girls. Or the dog. Or the other monkey. He concentrates.

Let us return, beloved aunt, let us return to my final adventures as a maid; to one of those three days and three nights I spent in the forest, eating roots and mushrooms and berries and chestnuts while performing womanly tasks, my dear, the tasks you taught me; I sewed the garments of my freedom in the glow of a small fire beneath the fat bough where two owls perched, and I looked down at the needle and cloth, then swiveled my gaze up and around, before and behind, because on the second night, alone and unarmed and without you, my aunt, under the minty shelter of the trees, I was afraid. Most afraid. I desperately longed to leave, yet I also longed for the safety of your skirts. I felt the slow and heavy breathing of a body that likely also feared, and then I saw the light from my little fire flickering in the eyes of an enormous bear, as enormous as the cathedral of Donostia, or so it struck me then. It was so close that I could no longer flee, although I was already fleeing. I sat still as a stone. And I lowered my eyes as you taught me a maid must do; I knew it then, how to be a maid. Today, however, I am a man, and so I was called in the convent that became my prison in Lima. You can imagine the reticence, and the lack of it, among the sisters. But wait, wait a moment, and I shall recount this episode of my tale. I am remembering now the wild thrashing of my heart and a warmth between my legs that I couldn't place until I heard the bear taking its leave. When I managed to stand, I chattered with the chill of my own urine and you weren't there to console me as you always had and I looked up and saw the light in the eyes of the bear that, taking its leave, had turned back to look at me; I saw that it was letting me live, the beast was leaving me with my life. It seared me, that gaze, broke something in me, lay down a bridge that met the man I am today. Not the girl I was, I did not understand, I could not see the bridge, I could not see forgiveness, in the bear was nothing but a threat receding, its back declared another chance to me; another door opening. And I could only faint in silence, which is like dissolving. Like metal melting, thus I fell, and I lay prone on the ground by the fire, waking at times and yearning for someone, for you, to accompany me. I feared they never would, that the cost of roaming freely would be the distance between me and all others, the distance that would permit me to keep my secret, and then I believed that in the eyes of that bear I had somehow looked into the eyes of God; I did not see the bear, my dearest, I saw God in its eyes, as if the bear was not the one who had let me live. And I believed myself accompanied; he protected and kept me, he volunteered the keys that opened doors, and bears that forgave, as I made my way forth. Do you believe it was God? Do you believe it? Was the bear a mere instrument? Today I believe the bear was a bear, but in it was also something of God, as there is in everything and everyone. What is memory, how can it be that I return to myself, to what I was, to what I smelled, to what I touched, to what I saw, and how is it that I find so much I had not found before? If I did not find it before, then is what I tell you true? I know not how, but if I am here it is because the bear wished to let me live, although I did not know it then.

Let me tell you of the bridge that a bear laid before a girl so that a man might cross it. It must be so, that we are offered bridges over which we cross seas, rivers, streams, entire oceans only later. Must the bridge of the novice be crossed by the muleteer? God willing. He must have wished for me to go, for had He wished otherwise, I would not be here now, I trust you will agree. It may be as you say, that nothing is written, but it could not possibly be if He did not wish it; is this not so, dear aunt? As for the bridge, I didn't see it, for my mind was yet dark, obsessed with fear, obsessed with the zeal for flight. When I woke from my fainting, I didn't notice the small grasses before my eyes, nor the embers, still red, within reach of my hand, nor even my hand, the soft plump hand of a young maid; I conveyed it to the needle and thread and sewed my garments with my eyes fixed on my fingers. Perhaps I understood that my sole weapon was a needle, your needle, and I would need to make all possible use of it. I finished the clothes and had to put them on without the aid of a mirror, I had no choice but to trust in my handsomeness and walk with long, firm strides; to advance, doing all that I was not allowed to do in my girlhood years; I made myself a man by obeying you, yet in the opposite direction. Do you see? I had not set eyes on many men before; the men of God, above us at the pulpit, and my father and the others, from afar, sitting still at mass, no more. I did not even remember seeing my own elder brothers. I was an inverted maid for part of my journey, until I met enough men to become one, dear aunt, myself.

10

Antonio stopped in the center of the square, standing before his former cell. And let out three shouts. With the first, he summoned two platoons. They emerged, immediately and in formation, from the barracks. Tired of the captain's furious comings and goings, they obeyed, relieved, his orders to depart in search of priests, peering under rocks if necessary. With the second shout, he sent a hundred soldiers to gather flowers and another hundred to dip tallow candles and clean the church. With the third, he called for fine raiments. He couldn't believe his luck. It was the morning of the day he'd been condemned to death by hanging. In an hour, if it hadn't been for his dreaming and his singing, he'd have been sent to trudge, shackled at the ankles, hands, and neck, in the tragic line of villains, to the gallows. Instead, he was off to the river. He passed the barracks gate and stepped into the jungle. He felt the cool air in the damp, dense shade of the trees. The path was narrow and furrowed with roots and vines, but easy to tread, demanding only basic attention. To watch where you step. When he reached the bank, he draped his new clothes over a branch. He stripped off nearly all his rags. Antonio never forgot the eyes that may be watching. The water embraced him, warm and transparent. He let himself go. Surrendered to the pleasure of the day. Instead of advancing toward death, he was swimming with the dorado that leapt like fleeting comets and the striped surubí that escorted him as if he were a king. Black-bodied, white-collared toucans surveilled him. Where were the priests? The magpies cried in their bright voices. The leaf frogs descended from the treetops to submerge themselves. Up above, the vulture studied the bare beast splashing. And the nearby she-jaguar that lucky Antonio had failed to notice, a tranquil scrap of sun with spots of night, her placid eyes on the water and on her wading cubs, as she sat on the rich red earth and licked her claws postbanquet. This one's mine, the vulture thought. Serenely, it lit into what remained of the poor tapir that had lost its life with the breaking day, just like the bishop, celebrating the change of fare. It had wearied of eating men and women and children. Antonio felt the fresh water, the freshest he'd ever felt against his skin and in his mouth. And he understood that everything is true beneath the trees. He understood all things, as fruit on the tongue is understood, light in the eyes, everything touched with the hands. This time, he vowed to himself, he wouldn't ignore the sheer vividness of living as he had always ignored it once he grew reaccustomed to being alive as a sure and certain thing. And chanced it all on cards or war or garments. Antonio likes dressing finely, the fine Spanish gentleman that he is. It was getting late. He emerged from the water and made his way toward the new clothes shimmering among green leaves. He had to organize fatuous, memorable funerals for the condemned and for the baptized Indians. He looked up at the blue sky and the brown river and the red earth and the green jungle. He felt happy to be breathing. He knew he had the Virgin of the Orange Grove to thank for it, and, as saving lives is much to the Lady's liking, he decided to speak with his captain and ask him to pardon the other prisoners. "Other" no longer: just prisoners. To save them, as his lordship the bishop would undoubtedly have wished, had he known his death was imminent, too quick for him to confess his paltry sins; this is what Antonio must tell his superior. Perhaps the Lord, in His infinite mercy, would consider a good deed done in His name when Judgment rolled around. Antonio was tangled up. He'd knotted himself in his clothes as he was putting them on. And he shook free, chuckling, saying aloud the bit about the paltry sins, so that he'd be able to repeat it later, with due solemnity, to his captain. How hapless of the bishop to have died without a priest beside him! He put on his shoes. They fit well. He put on his doublet, as if it had been sewn for him alone, his jerkin, and his ruff. Now he was a proper lord. He felt equipped for command. He'd suggest that the captain decree there should never be fewer than two priests at hand, and if one were off evangelizing or carousing, then the other should stay on guard, obligated to make his rounds, so that no one, much less a man as holy as the bishop, could possibly die unconfessed. He walked back to the barracks completely oblivious to the snakes. He was practically dancing, zigzagging like the girl in his dream. With a little hop, he lifted his right leg, crossed it over the left. He set it down again. Another little hop, he lifted the left, crossed it over the right. And so he advanced, a cheerful dancer. Close to the fence, he set down both feet and began to march. Right-left. Right-left. About face, forward march. Both legs straight and moving forward. Antonio, toy soldier, hard as wood, off to see the captain. With manly martial strides, he crossed the threshold. And was forced to change his plans. There on the gallows bucked the ten villains with whom he'd spent the previous day and their final night. Their whole bodies arching. Sketching a violent C to one side and the belly of a D to the other in a desperate struggle to retain their lives. They didn't want to perish. Poor little bodies. They'd expended all their strength, a lifetime's worth, in the briefest spurt of resistance. As they should. No time to spare for any thereafter. Poor imprisoned bodies. Hands bound. Bagged heads. And the rope around their necks as the only support.

He was certain that if they'd had their faces to the wind, he would have seen the very same hanged man thrashing in ten barely distinguishable bodies. Some slightly thinner. Some slightly fatter. Some slightly darker. Some slightly paler. Some slightly taller. Some slightly shorter. Dressed in ragged finery or in ragged rags. But all with the very same face washed clean by so many tears, tears that had smelted their features over the long night of weeping. He'd managed to sneak a glance at them when he stopped by after his chat with the captain, and so they remained: the same sole man, no longer either white or brown, poor or rich. A kind of amorphous mass, scarcely differentiated. A near nothing. Perhaps the eve of the end and the breath of death in the throat achieved what no one ever could: the true equality of mankind. But it must be said that of the truly rich, down in the dungeons, there were none. The rich seldom commit punishable crimes. He wanted to laugh, but laughter was bitter to him before the gallows. It must have been the Virgin of the Orange Grove working another miracle: he pitied them. Or perhaps he pitied himself—he should have been there too. Faceless. As near to nothing as the rest. Kicking in vain, only to die regardless.

His head was elsewhere. Partly there, accompanying the fate of his former fellows, but more absorbed with questions of why this one had met it, and this one too, but not that one. Besides, if he was to remain separate from the prisoners still tussling with their death as it overtook them, he'd better start thinking about how to get far away from here. And change his name and his features and his village of origin and his trades. Oh, his head was absolutely elsewhere. That wasn't good. He'd promised the Virgin he would save the condemned and he'd already failed her by lingering too long by the river. He made her a new promise. He had to look upon the dying and think about them as he looked. But he soon began to think that crimes harbored their own direction, each crime its course, depending on who'd committed them. White or Indian. Rich or poor. Leading to the noose and the pyre or to the throne and the treasury. Two men could commit the same crime together: one would end up on the pyre and the other much better off than before, daubed in the drool of adoration. Object of praise and bronze statues. Crowned in gold. The direction of the offense, where it gallops like a sprightly steed, Antonio calculated, is the product of two factors: one, the cradle of the crime, the worldly place occupied by its perpetrator; and two, the might of his enemies. He felt a pang and liked to think, on account of his Virgin, that it was meant for his fellows in extremis. In truth, he wasn't sure if the pang was for them or for himself. How to tell. Maybe it was for both. He'd never wondered if hanged men's heads are covered to spare them the spectacle or to grant them a final space of intimacy. Perhaps there was a different motive altogether. The Spaniards weren't the sort to spare any vicious pomp or grant anything but confession to prisoners on the brink of death. Not even a last supper. Although they'd had one. And they'd eaten it all. The villains' appetite was a sight to behold. His too, when he was still condemned to death alongside the others. But what about the hooded heads—what were they for? He'd have to ask the captain as soon as he managed to snap out of his reverie.

He felt indebted to his Virgin of the Orange Grove. Since he couldn't save his fellows, he'd stay put until their souls departed, leaving their lifeless remnants behind. And there he was again, pondering anything but the matter at hand. They weren't pleasant to look at. Their poor suspended bodies grappled still. Antonio had already thought about everything he needed to think about. He was getting bored. And some took so very long to die. They must have been the youngest, who tend to be, when push comes to shove, the most foolish. Or maybe not: maybe a viceregal envoy was galloping forth bearing absolution, and the young men were refusing to resign themselves. Holding out until the envoy arrived. They wanted fifty years. A single day. An instant more. But who could withstand the poor body's desperation as it dangles from a rope yanked tight around the neck for so long. Ah, what a relief: now only three were left jerking there, the closest ones. And now, Antonio resolved, perking up at last, no distractions, not even for a second. But a passerby remarked that they were three murderers, three deserters, and the other four were found naked and most engrossed, en masse, in sinning against nature. His prisoners were fortunate. Sodomites are usually sent to the pyre. After all, according to the Bible, the scent of flesh consumed by fire shall appease Yavhé.

That fire. The great blaze. The greatest bonfire he'd ever known. The blaze of the New World sodomites that had brought such ills upon the Empire. Storms on the high seas. Pirates. Lost wars. King Philip II himself, God hold him in His glory, penned a letter to the viceroy and urged him to be less lenient. To forswear his benevolence. His tolerance, we might say. Might the viceroy be a pederast? Anyone can be anything, Antonio told himself again, and remembered the king's words to his viceroy. Who was the viceroy of all those present. Even those ignorant of his existence. The viceroy of all men and women. And the toucans. And the mushrooms with their little hats. And the pindó palms as well. And it goes without saying that the king's viceroy was also the viceroy of all the gold and silver. The spices and the diamonds. Albeit only by delegation of the king, who'd seized the quill with his own hands to write:

… if we consider that our daily tribulations are conveyed to us by the Lord Our God for these and other grave sins of Christendom that

stanch the course of His mercy, punishing us with incidents lately afflicting the treasure derived from those provinces, some lost in great quantities from the keeping of our nation, and others to the peril of storms; and if we consider likewise the most unfortunate occurrences endured by my armies at the hands of our multitudinous foes, it is most evident to myself and to all others that our Lord has become wrathful, and that He must have permitted the abovementioned and most continuous failures as punishment for our sins; and I have therefore elected to request, as I am so doing, that you procure, with great diligence and care, the public punishment of sins such that they shall stir great commotion across the republic, and such that every instance of said punishment may effect the necessary correction of wicked customs amongst all persons without exception …

All had read the letter. And reread it. At pulpits and in brothels. In courts and in fairs. On roads and in confessionals. In cities and in deserts. In convents and in barracks. And in the Indian villages. Even the villages of those Indians who don't know how to speak as God wills. Antonio was distracted again. Two prisoners were still shuddering mutely. Their silent death so distant from the howling demise of his early companions in American revelry. He wept at the sight of them. His Highness Philip II offered discounted taxes to the purest cities. Everything blazed. So did Cotita de la Encarnación. The mulatto man who was a slave girl in the shop of his first master, at the start of his shopkeeping life. Cotita who had tended him in his first American plague. Cotita who hoisted the heavy parcels of fabric. And with the same hands stroked his brow to check his fevers. Cotita who helped him hide his menstrual cloths. Cotita who sang in the shop and on the road. Cotita who danced with her head wreathed in flowers. Who called him my soul. My life. My love. And laid a garland of crystalline laughter around the days,

days identical except for the Lord's, days of selling and buying, haggling and granting credit and jotting down each item, each little thing, adding or subtracting each coin in the shop's great ledger book. He never understood what Cotita the African was laughing about, sweet girl, his first American friend. But her laughter was beautiful, Cotita's was. Dead on the pyre. Fried alive, Cotita. A bonfire on every corner, in every square, at every town hall. Even the angels' wings had charred. The Catholics felled entire forests to purify their ledgers. They beheld each other with flames in their eyes and torches in their hands. One day they noted that Indians and Africans were scarce. Purity grew more expensive than taxes. And there was no change in the king's luck, or his kingdom's. It remained afflicted by Holland at sea. And by rebellious Catalonia. And by independent Portugal. Yavhé was unappeased by the stench of so much flesh consumed by fire. Or else other kingdoms did more burning.

Again he thanked his Virgin of the Orange Grove for reminding him of his promise. And for allowing him to skirt, in the nick of time, the feet dancing wildly in midair, spraying urine. Although he did catch a bit of spatter. It seemed to be his fate, getting spritzed by the piss and defecations of these folk, even when his luck had turned. Antonio wept, as his cellmates had done before him. The captain approached.

"Enough weeping, you milksop. Concern yourself with the funeral of the bishop I have commanded you to organize."

"Forgive me, my lord, very well, your lordship, it shall be a grand funeral, most grand, rest assured, your grace, I weep, my lord, because one of these prisoners, your lordship, the one whose hood the vultures have plucked from his head, my lord, has an enormous aquiline nose, your lordship, just like my brother's nose, my lord, my only brother, your lordship, dead in a duel at the age of twenty-five."

Antonio half lied to his captain. The captain didn't care if he'd lied or why he wept. All he wanted was to put his secretarial talents to the test.

"To my offices, soldier."

Antonio snuck a final glance at his villains, now wilted flowers from head to toe, all listing downward. Dead flesh seeks the earth. The last thing known by a man or a woman, or even a very small child, is that they will be welcomed into the embrace of the earth, which will shelter them as a mother does. But then their bodies will no longer belong to them, as the hanged men's bodies are no longer theirs. The earth receives them as a cooking pot does ingredients. And makes new lives: its own, the entire Earth's. But that wasn't what Antonio thought as he marched steadily along, erasing with his shirtsleeves the traces of the tears he'd shed for Cotita, who wound up charred in the fire, along with another hundred and twenty fairies, who were actually greater in number, some said two hundred, but there were many exceptions, despite the will of the king. He marched straight, Antonio, for the captain's chambers.

11

A person goes to sleep one day and wakes the next, which is the only reason that the days appear to be carved discretely from each other. But they're not. Boundless, they advance without edges, beginning and ending wherever they please. Or nowhere at all. Unless one takes the sun as both beginning and end. Even so, they aren't separate. He must have learned this in the forest by the convent. In the battles of Araucanía. On the eve of the gallows he survived. He learns it now. Governed by the intermittent wakings of the girls, their capricious hungers, their ball games, their seed-pod games. Antonio surrenders. He devotes himself to sensing the passage of time like a river into which the sun rises and sets. A current. Like the one coursing through him this very instant, the jubilant tumbling into the letter he's writing to his aunt. He lets it sweep him along. How could he not. How to explain with earthly words that a ship sets sail from him, bearing him away. He sails, Antonio, in this writing that both is and isn't him. He's rocked by the singing. The breathing of the girls and the monkeys. The warm pulse of Red beside him. The horses' hoofbeats at an ever-greater distance. The jungle's music. The croaks. The roars. The buzzing. The trills. The sweet and acidic fragrances. And the words slipping from his fingers.

"Hey, che, Antonio."

Even sitting, he must lower his eyes to meet Mitãkuña's. Her cheeks are nearly russet now. She looks healthier. Antonio congratulates himself. Red also looks up at him. Both smile. The little dog with her whole mouth. The tip of the pink tongue at the dark edge of the lips, between the fangs.

"Now what is it?"

He slips a hand into his pocket and removes it again, full of pindós. He's spent days filling and emptying his pockets with these fruits. He's practically forgotten they can be filled with other things. The girl's white toothlets split the first.

"Your mama, where is she?"

"Far away, in Spain."

"Grandmama, do you have one?"

"No, Mitākuña. I have an aunt. And you, do you two have a mother?"

"Yes. And papa and aunts and grandmamas."

"Where are they?"

"Near, che."

"So why do they not come looking for you?"

"Because of your bad spirits. But they are near, very near. Spain, where is it?"

"Far away, beyond the sea. Would you like to play with the little balls?"

They would. They sketch the line. They dig the hole. They toss one in. The larger monkey grabs it and scampers up the silk floss tree with the smaller one. Red barks. The mare and her colt are only interested in drifting this way and that. They're trying to disentangle themselves. To find a way out of the thickets. Look at your troops, Antonio. The girls, the dog, the monkeys, so utterly escaped from death. Like him. Equally fugitives. Equally survivors. Except for the horses. One might say that mother and son were never elsewhere, they just lived in their own world of orchids and milk. Orchid, then, the mother. Milk, the son. He can't think of what to call the monkeys. He'll have to ask the girls the next time they interrupt him. Now that they're playing, he can write a little more. He wants to rock back and forth a bit. He continues with his letter.

My legs took on their own independent life, dear aunt, and my chest and back as well, so too my nose and very eyes. My body grew on will alone, and my hands throbbed, hardening in their struggle against hunger. For I had to nourish myself with chestnuts, beloved, as if my little hands, so precious to you, the hands you sweetly pressed in yours, had parted, sundered from you and from my daughterly and novicial life, at the mercy of the thorns encasing the chestnuts that were, save the mushrooms and the occasional root, all there was to eat along the road, which was not one road but who knows how many roads I wandered here and there, on the first of all the journeys I undertook, knowing what I was leaving behind, but not what I would discover ahead. Chestnuts are armed, inlaid with needles like tiny spears designed to defend their destiny as chestnuts, their volition to sink deep into the blind earth and then unfurl into the light, let themselves grow high into trees and feel their leaves feeding on sunlight. I must have consumed half a grove of future chestnut trees in those days, and the half grove bled my hands that healed, yes, now toughened with calluses. The future of those chestnut seeds was within me. And these hands were still soft when I reached Vitoria, because hands are fully forged in war and the labors of men, or so I believed back then. Or believed it later. For a long time I believed it.

"Mba'érepa?"

"What, Michī?"

"Mba'érepa?"

"What is she saying, Mitākuña?"

"She says why does he eat clouds."

"Who?"

"God, che."

"Because he likes them. Just as you like pindós, Michī."

"Mba'érepa?"

"Because he does."

"Why does he not eat oranges, che?"

"Because he hadn't yet created them that day."

"The lightning thunder was there already."

"What lightning thunder?"

"Mba'érepa?"

"What are the monkeys called?"

"Yvypo Amboae and Antonio."

"Well, well. I thought they were called Mitākuña and Michī."

"Mba'érepa?"

"Because of your monkey business, Michī. You must choose names for them."

"Tekaka."

"And the smaller?"

"Kuaru."

The girls laugh. Antonio succumbs to it.

"Poop and pee, che."

"Well, those are foul names you have chosen for such lovely monkeys. But no matter, we'll call them whatever you wish. Which is Poop and which is Pee?"

"Stupid you are. Tekaka is the bigger."

On the day I reached Vitoria, dear aunt, my hands were not as strong as they needed to be and I did not know where to shelter. I walked and walked without my body ever tiring of walking, as it hasn't yet tired, for I am a muleteer, as I have said, and I always know where I am going, but in those days I didn't know until I met Pedro de Cerralta, a scholar there, who commended my Latin, which I believed to be poor; a Latin fit for mass, he said, and soon I found myself duly attired and reading Saint Thomas. It was this Pedro who dressed me. He, I later learned, was married to one of my mother's sisters; I did not remember her, I must have seen her once as a small boy, but it proved unnecessary for me to lie that

I did not know her, as I had already lied about my name. Would you like to know the very first name I chose? Have you guessed it? Not Christopher Columbus, no, but Francisco, after the poor Saint Francis of Assisi, and Loyola, after Iñigo the general. And this was seen as a fine name fit for the fine young man I was, because no one found the name to be unusual, nor the lad in question.

Memory, as you well may know, is a thing of dislocations; one does not recall memories in sequence, nor does he recall everything he has lived, nor even what he believes he possesses, nor can he take for lost what he has lost indeed. Because, beloved aunt, how can I be sure, when I am alone, as I have been, and nonetheless I am also the animals in my company, we are all of us together, and of course they too remember, yet they do so with the wordless memory of beasts? How can I be sure, when memories cannot subsist on a walnut grove, on a church, on a kitchen hearth, or on other folk? When life flows forth as a river without banks does flow, a torrent that veers and errs, plunging wildly wherever the path shows least resistance, yet colliding and shattering against as many angular rocks as it may find along the slope? With this I mean to say that I remember things I could not possibly have seen when as a young girl I fled from you and when as a young boy I fled from Spain without knowing it yet, and found myself out in the forest, because gazing upon stars and trees and animals is something I learned much later. If I saw them then, I saw them as mere compass points, as cargo and shelter, as food or menace, yet who remembers? The boy newly birthed by your tales, by your key, by every stitch in his new garments, or this muleteer weighed down with cloth, who treads beside his beasts and warms himself against them through the nights, the nights that, as you must know, are sometimes cold and wet and . . .

"Hey, che, why does he not eat poop and pee?"

"Not again . . ."

"God, the papa of God."

"Mba'érepa?"

"He must not like monkeys, Michī."

"Nde japu! Real poop and pee, che."

"Because he hadn't yet created them."

"Mba'érepa?"

"Because he had not."

"Why do you not eat them?"

"Jatu, che. He does not eat clouds."

"Mba'érepa?"

"They are air, che."

"Does your mother bring you food?"

"No."

"Who brings it?"

"Ka-ija-reta, you do not know them."

"Who are they?"

"Jungle keepers, che. The spirit of the tapir, jaguar, yacutinga bird."

"Spirits bring nothing."

"Mba'érepa?"

"Because they don't exist, Michī. They are superstitions, things that Satan puts in your head."

"Satan, who is he?"

"Go on, talk a walk."

Michī stands, takes a step, then another. It's the first time Antonio has seen her walk on her own. And she disappears. As if swallowed into the leaves. As if now green. Two days earlier, she couldn't even hold her head up. She's recovering quickly. Or a silent jaguar devoured her. Or she has turned into a snake. Or a bird. A smooth-billed ani wings past. Blue, blue. He's heard that these Indians can do such things. Transform themselves into plants and animals. He doesn't believe it, so he follows: he wouldn't like it if a beast devoured her for lunch. Hard to locate a small child in the space that opens before him. She could hide behind any silk floss tree. Or inside a yvyrá pytá, a living tree with a hollow trunk. Or up in the canopy. Behind any snarl of climbing vines. Behind a güembé, one of those plants growing everywhere with leaves like enormous fingers, if hole-riddled, twenty-fingered hands existed. She couldn't have gone toward the palm grove; he would've seen her. He walks and calls her name. A güembé leaf shifts, way up in the crown of the yvyrá pytá. There she is: he feels her breathing. He climbs. There's a she-jaguar, golden as if sun-embraced. Stretched out on an enormous bough. Michī inside her light. Curled against her belly. They look like a star. It can't be. It isn't. Now he sees the little girl alone, climbing higher. He sits there, waiting for her to get bored. She gets bored. They climb down. She's exhausted. She hugs him. He sits her on his shoulders. Could he have a tropical fever? How could he have seen the little one with a tigress? He keeps writing, Antonio, and forgets about the fevers and the tigress.

Today I remember, beloved aunt, and this is why I'm telling you tales of things that did not entirely exist when I experienced them. Of this Cerralta there is little that comes to mind, save that he took an interest in me and I in him; he esteemed, he said, my readings in Latin, my diligence, and I his conviction that he was conversing with a boy, and his gifts. He feared death, Cerralta, he feared secretly that there was nothing beyond this world, or that the beyond would be unpleasant; this is not a memory, I only understand it now as I write these lines and eat fruits more luscious than any you have ever tasted, for this new world is old and has ancient trees and ancient jungles teeming with delicious things, I am helpless to describe these flavors, this riot of succulence that is the very essence of the New Indies. I wish to tell you about the fear of death, which made Cerralta suffer, and which I understand today, though I did not understand it in Vitoria so many years ago, when my uncle, who did not know that he was my uncle, would have me read to him again and again and seventy times seven more times the same words in Latin, those of Saint Thomas Aquinas, you must remember them, although they are not among your favored tales, for what most delighted you—do they still?—were accounts of the world, filled with oceans and ships and exotic beasts and towering trees and fruits bursting in a surfeit of juices and stars flitting about as birds do. And in concert, in unfathomable dances for the greater glory of the Lord Our God. Love of the world says yes, yet that was not what I read to Cerralta, who suffered from the fear of death, or rather of life after death. For that is what death amounts to, does it not, dear aunt? He would have me recite from the Summa Theologiae *on what the world will be like after Judgment Day, this I do remember, though not perhaps the words themselves: "All the world and all the stars in the sky were created for man, but when man has been glorified, no longer shall he need those influences and movements of the stars that now nourish life below; and this is when the movements of the stars shall then cease." Do you believe that all the world was created for men, even the stars in the sky? Might it not be that all the world was made for all the world? Or men for the stars? Or the stars for the trees and the trees for the stones?*

It was not easy for Cerralta to envision such a World of the Just with the stars unmoving: "Must it be so, Francisco? Are you reading what is written?" And he would take the book from my hands and have me translate every word, and then, yes, the world was augured to be far more luminous, so that men may see God, and Cerralta would nod his head: "Yes indeed, it is for this purpose that Judgment Day must come, so men may see the Lord Our God," he would assert with great confidence, for it consoled him and improved his spirits, and urge me to continue. When I asked him whether it might not be more fruitful to discuss matters of such gravity with a prelate, he replied, "My son, that is precisely what I have done, I have spoken with dozens of prelates, and so it happens that their answers are legion, and contrary, and their utterances rarely concur when it comes to the contemplation of Our Lord by the Just," and he urged me to read on, and I did so, for this was my duty. And when I reached the part that said, "There shall be no need for animals nor plants, for they were created to preserve the life of man, and man shall then be incorruptible," I asked him, "Do you believe, my lord, that the world must be so empty and so still?"

"Hey, che."

"What?"

Mitākuña claps a hand over his mouth and points up. A vibration. A rustle of air.

"Here it is. The lightning thunder."

"It is a hummingbird."

"A lightning thunder."

"What does the lightning thunder do?"

"Fire. It makes fire when it is angry."

"And when it is content?"

"It flies and eats from flowers, che. See it."

The bird, a miracle in its way. Iridescent. So quick and so still. It moves its wings so fast it can't be seen, and it hangs in midair until it vanishes. Into the blossoms.

That he didn't know was the very thing that told me, my dear, that he too was unsettled by the image of the deserted world, yet more unsettled still by the question of how bodies were to be resuscitated. Whole? With tongues for speaking? Might the Just need to speak as we mortals do in order to understand one another? And would we need understanding when we no longer need anything at all? And if the hand of a thief is cleaved as punishment for his sins, will it be restored to him in resurrection? And will the rib of Adam, from whence Eve was forged, become part of Eve or restored to Adam? And if—this notion caused my uncle great distress—we would have no need for appetites or births, since death would be no more, would the body resuscitate with its concupiscent parts already severed? Or merely useless?

Dear aunt, the old man grew uncouth. He squeezed his loins, swore he would never sin again, swelled where he squeezed, and continued to swear and beg God to forgive him, and then he fled. To the cathedral, I later learned, to confess. Such was the tenor of my early months in that place: books in the evenings and questions and more books and more questions and Cerralta imploring the Lord to save him from himself, as his eyes narrowed and dampened and he clutched himself tighter before dashing away. I realized it would be impossible for me to stay much longer, and I decided to wait for winter to pass, trusting that the chill would temper his fevers, but I was mistaken; my uncle's anguish and appetites grew only more desperate in the darkness and the snow.

But the first anguish, his fear of death, made him urge me to study so that I might answer his questions myself, which was not my wish. My wish was to roam, not become a man of letters; had I wished to sit still, I would have stayed with you, listening to your tales, governing at your side, wearing breeches beneath my habit. He did not want me merely cultured, his inclinations were otherwise, but I would rather spare you the pain of knowing the vices of your relations, for Cerralta was married to one of ours, of mine. It is enough to know—is it not?—that I fled before the end of winter, when he stopped absconding to the cathedral in horror at his own urges, and fell prey to his appetites, insatiable as they were, clamoring for new prey and setting their sights on me. I left his home, though not without taking some of his copper billons. Little by little, I had been losing my affection for him, and by the time I *was forced to bar my chamber door, I had none. Defending my honor would have cost me the life of roaming I had just begun; all I could do was pilfer what paltry coins I could find and depart, one stormy night, knowing that he also feared water, feared death by water and by lightning, and this fear was stronger than his passions, at least in the dead of January. I dared not risk the chance that February would see him overcome his fear of all but being satisfied.*

"Hey, che, Antonio."

"What is it now?"

"Who is Satan, is it you?"

"No, not I, Mitākuña. He is the fallen angel."

"What is an angel, che?"

"Well … a messenger of God. Angels are like men with wings."

"Where do they live?"

"In the sky, with God."

"You saw them?"

"No, almost no one can see them. Only the chosen can."

"Like Ka-ija-reta."

"No, it is different."

"Nahániri."

"Mba'érepa?"

"Because the Bible says so, Michī. The word of God."

"Mba'érepa?"

"Would you like some ubajay?"

"Blech, che, go find another thing."

"Go find it yourselves. And go off singing, so I know you're safe even if I cannot see you."

Swiftly I happened upon a muleteer, dear aunt, one like myself, who agreed to take me for a few reals along with his cargo, a cart packed to bursting with hay and hens. I remember, truly this time, that they laid some eggs, and we ate these eggs and cheese on the road when we were not resting, the hens and muleteer and I, beneath the blankets. I remember they were long and many, the leagues that delivered me from La Vizcaya for the first time, and black and orange the hens; their feathers clung to my garments and made me cough, and the muleteer laughed as I now laugh, writing you this letter in my own hand, and the butterflies stir from their slumber this morning, clustered on the boughs of the trees and the vines. I am very still, and my animals are still, all of them, my mare, her colt, my dog Red, I don't believe I have mentioned her yet, how strange, but there will be time. We are all still, and charmed; the butterflies have come. You have never seen so many, I had never seen so many until yesterday, first there were a few, then more, and then I found myself enveloped in a cloud of butterflies as large as fists and small as bees, some black and orange and others blue and some green and others red and others violet. We found ourselves enveloped in a cloud of their brisk flitting, so different from the flight of birds. They flutter, butterflies, rising and falling and pausing in the ether, and nonetheless they advance, immersed in the yellow air, and their wings glimmering among the leaves and branches of the jungle; they reflect the sun, which turns to velvet, the air softens, and all other things with it. They drift this way and that, from flower to flower, and dusk falls and they began to alight in the silk floss trees and the pindó trees, and the latecomers also arrive, those who do not fear the cold and move unhesitating toward one par-ticular bough among all the many boughs so dense with butterflies, and when they are on the verge of alighting among the rest, there seems to be no room, no space left for even one more, and then they do hesitate; they beat their wings for several instants in the air, as if in fear of snapping the branch, and such a thing seems impossible under their infinitesimal weight, and yet, beloved aunt, you should *see the branches warp toward the ground under the mass of them. As you should see the ground itself covered in butterflies, because there are also butterflies that die here.*

Do you think that the World of the Just could exist without trees or animals? Sheer stone? A desert, my dear, an incommensurable desert, made of rocks alone, all naked and scorched by the sun. Could Saint Thomas be mistaken? So Cerralta would often have me believe; he said what I have written, dear aunt, I remember it well.

He jumps. Tekaka has leapt onto his neck. Tosses a branch to his feet. It's packed with bordó fruit, yellow, orange, red. Small. Kuaru begins to eat them. Antonio brightens. The taste is mild, refreshing. He eats some more. The girls' voices approach. They sit around the branch and bite into the fruit.

"Hey, che, this is not also your orange, Antonio."

"Mba'érepa?"

"Because it is a pytangy, Michī."

12

Perched in the shadows of his office, the captain bit his nails. The candlelight lanced wickedly across him, illuminating the bald spot beneath his sparse mat of hair. Beyond, the royal coat of arms and the gilded crown, embroidered into tapestry, framed him with gold and pearls. Antonio winced at the beam that bounced off the bare pate of the captain, who glanced up, trying to understand what was wrong with this idiotic secretary who'd failed to obey his command.

"Enter, imbecile."

Antonio stepped toward the table, heaped with papers written in the elegant imperial calligraphy. Strong words decreeing life for some and death for others. Gold for some and hunger for others. His right eye was wounded, trickling. And he wondered if his captain burnished his entire dome before combing his hair over it each morning. And with which ointment. How coquettish, his captain, and how bellicose. It's gun oil. Antonio was impressed, but he bowed his head and took the remaining steps toward him. Imbecile, the captain bellowed once again. Antonio feared offending his superior, but his hands rebelled. Defended his nostrils from the stench. He closed his mouth to keep from vomiting. The captain stood. He seized the candlestick, obscuring the imperial coat of arms, and shed light onto two shapes under black blankets. He removed the cloth. Antonio understood. There stood two cages. In one, a fat monkey, a thin monkey, and a skeletal monkey, dead. In the other, a small creature, slender as wire. Michī. Her bones blanched her skin. The captain spoke with sorrow in his voice.

"What you behold is all that remains of a great man and a fine friend, the holy bishop. His sole bequest! Vanity of vanities! His entire life—and what is left?"

Antonio beheld what was, apparently, left. Creatures and monkeys in cages full of flies and excrement.

"It is an experiment, the bequeathal of the prelate, who was a man of science. He performed many experiments. He devoted his life to worshiping the Lord. Through experiments, dear Ignacio, he always said to me, we come to better know the world that He has made. And to know His creation is to worship it." The captain stopped short. Collected himself. He nonetheless released, under his breath, a fervently emotional "O my dear friend."

One more small silence. And he continued.

"The bishop knew quite well that Indians have souls, though it may not be evident, good secretary—just look at this one. Just as the resurrection of Christ is hardly evident, and yet it remains the sublimest truth in all the world. What the prelate did not know was whether these jungle dwellers had a head. Of course he could see them, their heads. But he did not know whether they used the head they carried on their shoulders, and he likewise doubted whether they had a head for hierarchy, as monkeys do. The dead one is the foot soldier, the scrawny one the second lieutenant, and the fat one the captain. The bishop judged that capuchin monkeys could have an army if they wished, that is, a kingdom, gold, and laws. By contrast, these human vermin could not organize themselves even while dying of hunger and thirst; they insisted on distributing their crusts and droplets equally. The other two nearly died. Or else they died and he gave them a Christian burial. I cannot say. What kind of intelligence is that? All of them dead, where one might have lived. Those jungle Indians, they cannot do sums," the captain ruefully concluded. Although he added, brightening at once:

"The jungles are ours."

"My lord, without a doubt, your lordship, we have defeated and shall defeat these and all others who dare resist the force bestowed upon us by God so that we may propagate his Holy Name across the entire Earth and save the souls of the savages for His Kingdom."

"And for our own, good secretary," the captain chuckled. Antonio echoed him.

"So how does the experiment end?"

The captain wasn't sure, and alas, he no longer had his friend around to explain. It was a day of great grief; he couldn't possibly think about it. Perhaps he'd leave the child in there. Perhaps he'd set her loose tomorrow. Perhaps he'd undertake some scientific experiment of his own. How does one raise a perfect servant, one who will never betray you?

"Even God was betrayed by His people, captain."

"Indeed, indeed. But God gave us free will. And I am no God and I give nothing for free."

"And the monkeys, must they be servants as well?"

"Do not be a clod. And stop distracting me. Go tend to your own affairs, secretary, and leave me to my science."

He ordered Antonio to busy himself with his papers while they waited for a platoon to come with a priest, who would then conduct a proper mass for the poor bishop, now reduced to worm food. Watch the cages, the captain also ordered: he won't have them stolen. Antonio was already sitting. And he ventured no other answer than: yes my lord. Of course my lord. As you wish your grace. Thinking what a numbskull, who would bother stealing Indians and monkeys? These new lands are full of both and anyone who would want them already has plenty. It would be like thieving branches in the jungle. He read all the papers, *the Virgin pure went walking from Egypt to Bethlehem.* He established an order. Mountain of requests from noblemen, *and halfway on the journey, the Child needed to drink.* Mountain of criollos. Mountain of sums of debits and credits. Mountain of promissory notes. Lordly sinecures. Orders from the viceroy and commanders. *Oh blind man, tell me, blind man, would you an orange give.* He worked and worked, most industriously. Almost accustomed now to the mephitic stench. What luck, that neither monkeys nor starving children make any noise. He was left with one more mountain, that of urgent matters. He faced the challenge of arranging them in order of priority, but which priority? *To soothe a thirsty child and bring him some relief.* Antonio heard himself singing and stopped. The thirst of this child. He hadn't kept his promise to the Virgin of the Orange Grove. He hadn't written the letter. Or stayed the execution. Or really accompanied his prisoners at all. The Virgin had made him see, and she'd saved his life. No kept promise could possibly suffice. Not to mention the future promises to keep. He'd have to make two promises. Or maybe three. Like the Three Marys. Which are three, neither one nor seventy. Well, he'd have to think it over. What he knew for sure was that there was a very tiny, very thirsty child inside the cage. Yes, the captain had made this quite clear. Antonio could bring her some oranges. A good idea. It cheered him. He resolved to find an orange tree. He'd better set out soon, as it would be no small feat to locate one in these jungles, dense as they were with wild and intoxicating fruits, but with few oranges and orange groves. How many oranges would it take to pay his debt? He sang again in his daytime voice, his tenor voice, following the verses toward an answer. *The Virgin, pure and righteous, reached out to pluck just three. The child, only a child, craved all that he could see.* The Virgin could make do with three, he reasoned. But the child craved all of them. He understood, with a sure and unwavering flash of certainty, that he'd have to obey the Child, who is God made flesh. Besides, the Virgin, who was the mother of that Child and all others in this world, the mother even of the most brutish Indians, would be glad to see her children provided for. He already had a plan: he'd bring the little girl to a forest of orange trees he thought he'd glimpsed in the middle of the jungle, some ten leagues from town, before the soldiers could set it on fire. Who knows how it got there, the grove. Some hermit with Spanish proclivities. Or a deserter. Or perhaps some other miracle had planted it in his path, granting him the perfect way to keep the promise he'd made to his Virgin of the Orange Grove. After the funeral, he'd drink with the captain, address him in Biscayne, and sing him songs from the motherland that he yearned for. Her green, green meadows. People speaking the tongue he dreams in. The captain's wife and the daughter with his eyes. He'd slip a somniferous herb into the noble chalice in case the man-at-arms didn't yearn enough. And in case the wine troubled his sleep. He'd take the child. He'd cut oranges for her to eat until she tired of them. And then he'd return her to the cage of the captain, who would slumber on, oblivious to the whole affair. Antonio would have kept at least the first of his promises to the Virgin. He finished his work. Stood up. Gave Michī a bit of water. She was frightened, but thirst got the best of her. He had to tip it into her mouth. Antonio was very pleased. She was clearly dying of thirst. What the captain had told him was also clear. They'd never be an army. Never an empire. They'd never discover new worlds. Poor foolish Indians. Who could blame him and his people for conquering the likes of them?

13

The girls are flying, clinging to the neck of the star tigress. The tigress lunges at Antonio. Claws spread. Teeth bared to the wind. Roaring. He feels her tongue on his face. Sword in hand, he lifts his arm to slay her. He was dreaming, he realizes. He sees her just in time. In an instant so brief it barely exists, he manages to contain his might. The dull sword slashes some branches near Red, whose face hovers close to his. She flashes her teeth, having sensed the initial violence of his gesture. Now she sees the risk is gone. Her tongue was what woke him. His whole face lapped and sticky. From the ground, Antonio finds round, startled eyes fixed on him, the dog's arched lashes, Mitākuña, Michī, Kuaru, and Tekaka. The only ones who seem to expect nothing are Orchid and Milk, who pick their way along the riverbank. As soon as they notice them, the capybaras—their semispherical bodies, their deft little hands—freeze right where they are. One is craning its neck toward some weeds. Another has its little foot in the air. Another, both little hands caught in the act of lifting leaves to its mouth. Since the horses don't stop, seeking a path to tread, the smaller creatures choose to stampede straight into the river. Plop, goes one of the largest. Plop, plop, plop, go the smaller. Plop, the other big one.

Mitākuña speaks.

"Hungry, che."

"Antonio, not 'che.' I have mare's milk for you."

"Blech, che, Antonio. Make fire."

And she goes off with Red. Antonio gathers branches, leaves, dry seeds. Blows briskly on the embers. The girl returns with a terracotta pot filled with enormous eggs, pale blue with black spots—what kind of bird?—and fruits. Mitākuña presents the pot to Antonio, who understands he's supposed to cook. He boils the eggs. Sets two in each coconut bowl. He splits the fruits and doles them out in equal portions, including Kuaru and Tekaka. He gives a raw egg to Red. They eat together around the fire. Mitākuña and Michī seem to hear something. Could be voices. The Indians. Close by. Or far away. Close, Antonio surmises, judging by the pot and eggs, he hasn't slept much, he's been writing so feverishly to his aunt, but he can still reckon distances. A pot of eggs is clear evidence that they're close. Or not. They could have delivered the pot and departed again. What does he care, so long as they keep sending food. The girls' voices are sweet. Like a soft touch when you thought you'd die alone. That's how sweet. They move their feet and little heads. They sing. Their cheeks have filled out a bit. They aren't ugly. They're lovely. Antonio beholds their faces, their hands, their rounded bellies. They're getting better quickly. And they could do with a bath. He'll take them when they seem tired. They'll put up less resistance. He's right. When the moment comes, they don't complain. He carries the smallest in his arms. She's still a bit frail. Or he's just gotten fond of her. In the river, he supports her head and the base of her back. Michī splashes her arms and legs. She shoos away the boga fish that flash in and out of sight like rays of sun, rippling water that would be green if it weren't perfectly transparent. She laughs and splashes Antonio; she splashes the monkeys, who stream water over their own heads. When they return to shore, she clutches Antonio's neck with both hands. She hugs him. She smells like a puppy. He doesn't know how he knows: when has he ever stopped to smell a puppy, a baby? But it's a puppy smell. Orchid and Milk wander off. The riverbank. That small strip without foliage. They'll roam. He's not sure if he should tether them. No. That would make them easy prey for any other beast. He'll need them later. He'll look for new ones if they go, he thinks. Red, who didn't even dip a paw into the river, joins the contingent, wagging her tail. They make their way toward the fire. Antonio collects more fronds and branches. Rests them against a vine that traces a circle a few steps from the roots of the yvyra pytá tree, which has served as a chair so far. He uses a hard branch as leverage to uproot a stump. They move to a new tree. This one will be better for napping. It's hollow and inside there's cool air, which can't be found anywhere in the jungle but in these trees. How hard he's worked. How it aches, his back. How the sweat trickles into his eyes. How the bees throng him, ravenous for salty water. How the mosquitoes and barigüí flies assail him. How is it that he's ended up like this, tending to little girls, walking among insects of all stripes? Mitākuña helps. They arrange a circle of stones in the center of the house. Antonio brings the embers. They have a table and a fire. Tomorrow he'll make the door. This is good, Antonio thinks. Lunch will come. He rests his back against his tree chair. The inkwell on the new table. He starts to write.

I thought I would lose my hands, dear aunt, on the road to Valladolid. It was so cold that we all slept, even the hens, huddled together beneath many blankets, the largest of which served as a roof below the leather sheet to trap the heat, the smallest swaddling us like caterpillars in their sheaths. We too slept, the muleteer and I, beneath the hens and with hens between us and with hens roosting on our backs. Do you know how warm a hen can be in wintertime? And thirty hens? And have you ever noticed that the gazes of fowl always seem nervous? It must be due to the placement of their eyes on either side of their heads, which they have to swivel about in order to see. Owls, also birds, whose eyes face front, look more serene.

A young hen took a shine to me, following even when I went off and tended to my private needs. Respectful, she always stood guard, shifting her head from side to side and taking little steps, leaving me a yard of intimacy, yet as soon as I lifted my breeches and emerged, she came running, crazed, flapping her wings, moving her legs as quickly as her head, or perhaps the head more than her legs, rising up in momentary flight, disorganized and comical, as is the way of hens. After a spell, I stopped to play, pretending to chase her, then she to chase me, and I liked to weave my fingers through her feathers, and she brooded on them as if they were her eggs, and I believe that is how I made it to Valladolid with ten fingers intact. Now that I recall her, recall all the hot air she harbored in her plumes, I wonder whether hens barely fly because their feathers are so useful for this other task, and I tell this to myself, and wonder why I am given to thinking that one part of the body must exist to do a single thing to the detriment of all the rest. The solitary man thinks a great deal, he who travels with his beasts thinks a great deal indeed, however much he also sings, and reads, and writes letters to his aunt.

"Hey, che."
  "What."
  "And Satan?"
  "What about Satan?"
  "Who is he?"
  "A bad angel, Mitākuña."
  "He has wings?"
  "Yes."
  "What color?"
  "White. No, no, red and black."
  "Nde japu! They are orange, che."
  "Mba'érepa?"
  "Because he is not real, Michī."

"He flies?"

"Yes."

"Fast?"

"Faster than the lightning thunder, Mitākuña."

"He makes fire, che?"

"Many fires. Hell is a lake of fire."

"Hell, what is it?"

"The place where sinners go after death."

"Singers, who are they?"

"Have you brought the fruits?"

"Nahániri."

"Well bring them, then."

I am astonished by this hen, flaring into my memory in full detail, as if out of nothingness, something illuminates her after all these years, wresting her from the dense fog of oblivion, and now I see her as if right before my eyes, as if she could shelter my hands in her plumage at this very moment. I am astonished also by the blossoms of the chestnut trees appearing in my mind, birthed there like chicks cracking through their shells, I can nearly see them, first the tip of the crest erupts, pink, dense pink, but pink with a bit of the blue from Spain, everything rushes back into my thoughts with a faint bluish tint, even white, even orange, even yellow, my dear, but then I see the tiny petals one by one, as if they were a trickle of milk and each petal a droplet; here is the entire crest, and at last the shell is reduced to nothing and the chestnut tree appears, bedecked, as people adorn their trees during the festivities there, I see the flowering chestnut tree and the entire chestnut grove festooned with garlands as if for a courtly ball, or like the sky at night, all full . . .

Fruit falls to his feet.

"There, che. Why is he bad?"

"Satan?"

"Yes."

"Because he refuses to obey God. And he tricks men so they will sin and go to hell."

"Mba'érepa?"

"Because he does not like to be alone, Michī."

"I also do not like that. You?"

"Sometimes I do. Like now, for instance. Would you let me keep writing, please, Mitākuña?"

... of stars. Spring came early to Valladolid, and this I do not remember, but I must have beheld the chestnut grove thinking of you; that was the first time it flowered without us looking upon it together. I bid farewell to my little hen, who traveled on to her new home, along with the others who had always been her companions. They were an inheritance, what was left of a man, those beautiful hens. Who knows what will be left of me, beloved aunt. The convent will be left of you. And I, perhaps.

14

He went to make sure that the great bishop's funeral was duly magnificent. The light pained him after several hours in the gloomy office. And his right eye still stung from the lightning bolt reflected off the captain's bald pate. He resigned himself to having one eye for the rest of the day. Still, before he'd crossed even half the square, he could see the church jammed with flowers. The silky petals sought their return to the sun, straining desperately toward the door and the bell tower. He wasn't sure that such barbaric blossoms, fleshy and sensual as sexes—yellow, fuchsia, violet, turquoise, azure—were entirely becoming of a solemn rite. Their greasy veins. Their fulgent sepals. Their inner petals caked with pollen. Their intense labella. They were all incitation, these flowers, all beckoning, colorful turgidity and lust. Entering the church amid the flickering of a thousand candles, he found chalices brimming with flowers. Cheerful bees sipped and buzzed. The greenish rainbows and voracious beaks of hummingbirds thrummed like apparitions. Tiny red black-masked frogs croaked occasionally, punctuating their placid rest. They filled the church with jungle. It wouldn't have surprised him had mass been officiated by capuchin monkeys. The church was ready for the pagan wedding of an unfaithful prince. He heard a commotion. Ten priests arrived. Bells clanged. The cloud of bees, hummingbirds, and frogs fled the church, hovering for an instant between the portico and the bell tower. The air shuddered. And split. It was a stampede of every color in the sky's diaphanous blue, and it seized the attention of all those present as if a dancing ghost had manifested. Antonio shut his mouth. Chewed two flies. Focused. And called for the bishop to be brought forth on the palanquin he'd ordered upholstered in lustrous black cloth, embroidered with gold-threaded crosses by the most skillful of Indian women. In parade dress, with martial gait, eight soldiers advanced, bearing His Holiness's heft. The music commenced, harps strumming "Ave Maria." Although it sounded more like the music of the rivers around here. The Indian child singers harmonized their voices. All attendees felt as if they were hearing the Child singing in Bethlehem. A gray smudge in the sky approached apace, looming imminent. It drew in the air, the greenest gleams of the entire jungle suffused with yellow beneath the leaden sky, and loosed a crack of lightning. The thunder silenced all other noise. Releasing a tremendous weight, the rain began. Assembled in the atrium, the ten little priests stopped singing, huddled together. They hushed the choir and hastened down. Five hid in the confessionals. The other five fell to their knees. Thunder, as everyone knows, is the voice of God, and each of the ten feared ending up like the poor bishop, with one foot in hell. They took turns, springing into action, and absolved themselves of everything. Even the Jesuit who'd sinned with his own mother—against nature!— was forgiven with no penitence beyond two Lord's Prayers. Absolved, they returned to the altar. The Indian children sang. Antonio also sang. He stood. Knelt. Stood again. Kissed the soul beside him. He moved without thinking, knew it all by heart, like everyone else. Repetition is, or can be, solace. But he didn't need it. Or maybe he did: he was grieved by the flowers that had wilted in the time it takes for thunder to rumble after lightning. He believed they'd wilted partly from the sorrow of finding themselves bereft of bees, hummingbirds, and frogs. And even more from disgust. Six soldiers had even fainted.

And the captain general looked pale. The bishop stank, and all anyone could do was pray for the ten priests not to deliver ten sermons. The pit was dug. Now to wait for the marble, a slab engraved by Indians to mark the illustrious grave. With its tender angels and cross thick with flowers. Its birds and its fleshy ferns. Antonio was eager for mass to end. The copious supper. The sweet songs he'd sing to the captain. The silky narcotic dreams that would make him drowsy. The provisions he'd gathered for the road. The orange grove. And the little girl, whose thirst needed quenching.

15

He's been swaying for a while. He realizes it, leaning slightly back, when a tiger ant bites him. He understands that the jungle gives and the jungle takes away. It no longer unsettles him to surrender small parts of his body. He considers this. Concludes that he was never terribly unsettled. Had he been unsettled, his body wouldn't be as it is now. He returns to the ant bite. To the swaying that not even the pain could halt. To the music that moves him. What he hears is music. A constant singing. Made of one soloist and many others. Instruments that sound like water over rocks. A drumming on the earth. Antonio is vibrating. He doesn't know when the singing began. It's somewhat like the jungle's own music. Suddenly there. Sometimes he believes it hails from the east. Or the west. Or the south. Or from the north. He reasonably infers that it must come from the same direction as the food, and that he could locate the source if he wished to. He doesn't wish to. Like cherubim, these voices, albeit in the Indian tongue. The singers are the Indians of this jungle. They must be children. Or women with high-pitched voices. Songs of peace, he deduces. His little ones also sing. They know by heart what the choir is intoning. The song comes from all directions. Even from below, from inside the earth. They must be treading firmly. Or striking it with sticks. They use it as a drum. As an instrument. Like a darbuka, the kind he's seen Moors play in Seville. The whole ground throbs and Antonio, delighted, whistles. He likes it. He decides they'll sing every morning. He'll teach them some songs in Biscayne. This could be his new life. Singing with the girls in his country. Returning to Spain. Even to the convent with his aunt. They could live together there. Though surely they'd be bored, locked up with all the nuns, however pleasant nuns can be. He keeps singing instead. Then returns to his writing. Plenty of time to ponder what to do with his life. But he's not going back to Spain.

Palaces and cathedrals and courts and more palaces and sumptuous abbeys, my beloved aunt, and a roaring river, the Pisuerga, which gives Valladolid its green, burgeoning everywhere with tender leaves across the rough, arid plateau of Castille, though I was scarcely able to appreciate this at the time. The boy I was stood in awe at the softness of the marble, streaked with color that, I think I do remember this, though perhaps I invented it, looked to me like veins, almost like nerves, and he imagined the stone he touched had been long ago traversed by the trembling of some living creature, and he himself trembled at the sight of life hardened in this way. It is curious, my dear, that I should recall this part of what I've rarely remembered since; stopping to behold those streaks, those petrified nerves, I must have barely glimpsed the splendor of the power, more splendid than all else, that had marbled those walls and columns. The boy I was, who in this fresh fate called himself Alonso Díaz, or Pedro de Orive, I can no longer be certain, so many names have I borne, trembled faintly with his own desire, wholly seized with longing for the raiment of a nobleman. Many were my flaws, as I have said, and my voracious appetite for courtly garb was by no means the least of them. Greed is an excellent general, ready to fight every battle. Soon after, even before I expended the few billons I had managed to pilfer from the uncle who coveted me for himself, even believing I was a boy, I succeeded in convincing Juan de Idiáquez—do you remember him?—to make me his page, dress me as such, and bring me to live in the palace. An attendant to the king, the Pious, Philip III, who made our Empire great; yet no, not ours, no longer mine, although I myself did serve that king and he did make me a lieutenant.

"Does it hurt, che?"

"Does what hurt?"

"The fire of hell."

"Have you ever touched fire?"

"Yes, che."

"And did it hurt?"

"Yes, much."

"Imagine what it feels like over your whole body, then."

"Ayyyyyyyy."

"That's why you must not let yourself be tempted by Satan. Or you'll be bound straight for his kingdom."

"What is kingdom?"

"Well, the country of a king, like Spain."

"What is king, che?"

"The lord of all, chosen by God."

"Do all obey him?"

"Mba'érepa?"

"They obey, or else they are sent to prison or to the gallows or to the pyre. Now go on, go off with the monkeys."

Yet in those days the king and the empire were still mine, dear aunt, a king all blond and orange, and with a mustache most coquettishly trimmed, and a little chin jutting out as if preceding the rest of his face, like the chins of our Habsburgs, and neither so tall nor so robust nor so radiant in spite of all the gold he wore, and which surrounded him from floor to ceiling, have you ever visited that palace? He was, when all is said and done, a man, born as pierced by death as all the rest of us, as are the butterflies and the silk floss trees and my little donkeys and my horses and my fine mules and oh, my Red, who would have me cease writing these words, who is not content to be stroked by my one free hand, and wants me to look upon her as well; she must be tired of chasing butterflies. I shall continue for a while, as I still must tell you of the king.

He was not so tall, as I have said, nor so robust, but looked rather frail, with skin as translucent as the marble adorning his palace, and furrowed with veins that his skin failed to properly cover; he was bluish white, the Pious was, though his furrows did not resemble the vital circulation of a living creature, but the dark vessels of a death that patiently ate away at him. And despite his meager radiance, despite his stature and sickliness, being in his proximity was like approaching the sun or the blessing of God, because the body of a king is not a body—did you know this, aunt?—but thousands, millions of bodies, although the king is born and dies alone, as all the rest of us must also do, as does the caiman, as do my butterflies, on whose rough head they are pleased to alight, and perhaps the caiman cannot feel them, because its hide is too thick to feel such slightness, and its eyes do not see much of what happens along its back, yet the caiman seems content to take the sun as it blooms with blue and orange and green and yellow butterflies, crowned like a king, like the Pious, the man who commanded with his very gait, the whole of him imperative, an empire, the power itself of kings, with their full aura of metal, a precious metal that gleams and cuts, that can cut and save, a veritable aura Philip had, the likes of which I have never seen since, and I have met my share of powerful men. Being close to the king meant entering that aura, seeing oneself tinted with that light, bathed in power; I do not remember if I knew it then, yet how could I have failed to know it, if seeing and understanding were the same thing.

"Hey, che, Antonio."

"What is it, Mitākuña."

"What is country?"

"Men and women who live in the same place and speak the same language and have a king."

"The jungle is no country, che."

"No. Yes."

99

"Mba'érepa?"

"Because it is part of Spain, which is a country, Michī."

"No."

"Nahániri!"

"Yes."

"Jaguar, snake, and tapir do not want it. And we do not also."

"There will be war, then."

"You fight against us, che?"

"Against you?"

... perhaps the longing to speak with you. But let us return to the royal aura, to the king, I wish to say; the sight of him neither cut me down nor granted me another life than the one I was already living. Speaking later to his successor, Philip IV, was more favorable to me, although his favor meant merely leaving to me what was mine. However, anointed as I was by his power, I was reborn on parchment with his blessing; the king thus rendered me legitimate—I, who was born to nobility.

Here reigns the power of the jaguar and of the snake and of all the miracles around me. My very hands, have you ever seen a thing more miraculous than the perfect composition of hands? The might of this fire ant, so named because it is red, and bites, and which bears a twig several times longer than its own body, so as to carry on constructing life itself. Like me, like you, like each of us, and all of us together. My life, the ant life I once lived in the great anthill of the Court, was brief; I hadn't yet plumbed even a part of it, and I now remember people only by their office, and some, like secretary to the king, or the king himself, counted but one official, yet most had dozens if not hundreds, and there were innumerable offices. I doubted whether or not to stay much longer, though it would have pleased me to become an armored knight, which is the first destiny of pages, but one evening, jesting with another page outside the lordly chambers, I heard my father's

voice, and the guard announcing him with his full name and title.
In the time Idiáquez made him wait, which I imagine was short,
though it felt so long to me that I was frightened, I sought to shirk
his gaze, just glanced at him a bit as hens glance, with one eye only,
and I saw in him my nose, these eyes that are my own, the shoulders
I was bound by blood to bear, the sturdy hands and the grace befitting
a noble elder who once had sat me on his knee. He struck me as a man
of power, although today I realize he was not: his hair was white
and his footsteps timorous despite the fury that possessed him. I saw
in him more fury than pain or fear for my fate. My father spoke to me
of some trifle, and I replied, fearing he would recognize me and lock
me up as a nun for the rest of my days, but no; my father did not know
my face. Then I heard him speaking to my lord, telling him of me, his
daughter, who had fled the convent, and my lord pledged to help him
search for the girl, asking if she had a suitor of some kind, my father
doubted that she could, and in that very moment I was certain. I was
relieved that my father did not recognize me; the door I saw swing
shut at the sight of him was not in fact a door, but a lid, the cover to
my coffin. I believed that the grave of confinement would open, and
not even by your side, for he would no longer entrust me to you, of
this I could be sure, I was relieved...

"Nahániri same language."

"No."

"Mba'érepa?"

"Because they are yvypo amboae, Michī."

"Yvypo Amboae can conquer jungles and mountains and
seas."

"Nahániri!"

"Mba'érepa?"

"Because we have gunpowder and ammunition. But do not
fear. I will defend you. Sing."

... and I fled, though with no joy in my body, a tender animal that wishes to embrace what it loves, and one must allow it, my dear, this I have learned, this may be the only thing I have ever learned in all my years of living. It was restless, this animal I am, or rather was, and lacked, as I have said, the joy I felt in the early days of my flight, which further distanced me from you. I believe you would have known me. My father didn't recognize me because he didn't know me well, how else could a father fail to recognize his child? I left the palace, took my garments and the few coins I had gathered, slept at an inn, and joined up with a muleteer, the first to wake. He was bound for Bilbao, so I was, too. Do you see, dear aunt? Muleteers have always been of great help to me.

Have they gone, Orchid and Milk? Have they found their open plain? Are they galloping across it? Are they startling capybaras in the river? He doesn't know. It's been ages since they left. Time to sleep now. Red has curled up in his lap. Yes, a nap. A fine idea.

16

"What is the worst of all fates for an uncle?"

"To have a monkey for a nephew!"

They laughed and ate. Crammed with marvels, their open mouths predisposed them to good humor. Their guffaws culminated in thumps on the table that were crowned with jumps of the silver that were crowned by new guffaws, and so forth.

"And the worst of all fates for a nun?"

"I could not say. To be Hebrew?"

"To have a fever but no curé!"

"Would that not in fact be the worst of all fates for the bishop? Oh, my dear friend!" An immaculate linen cloth emerged from the shadows for the captain to dry his tears with. "Farewell, dear fellow, penitent cherub, groom of the lash, one-handed onanist. Farewell, beloved companion of songs and executions, of feasts and pyres, of masses and gallows, of baptisms and last words that, alas, you did not bestow upon me."

"Do not weep, my lord, but let us toast to his holy spirit, which must be enfolded now in the arms of our good God. And I implore you to heed these words, your grace: command the priests to request permission before they travel, so that no fewer than two are ever to be found in the settlement. And if one is out reveling or asleep, then the other shall keep watch, making his rounds like a sentinel around the preeminent homes. Under this system, no one shall die without absolution."

"Clever, very clever. Why, you really are most clever, my dear friend. I toast to your health, to your wealth, to buxom women!"

"To yours, my lord! What is the worst of all fates for fate itself?"

"Well, let me think—to find El Dorado when no one cares about gold any longer?"

"To fall into a haystack and get pricked by the needle!"

Silken, the night. Wine in the throat, tapir meat clinging between teeth. Tongues ecstatic with the sweetness of pineapple. The harp plucked like droplets dripping coolly onto rocks, onto the fine lace of green ferns that blanket, majestic, the entire ground. The conversation in Biscayne and the river's gentle course. What a beautiful supper! What bliss inebriated the captain and his new scribe! Tremulous candlelight shed its glow on them. Golden was the banquet. Their enormous noses, golden. Golden their four eyes when they leaned forward to behold their plates. And the goblets and goblets. What a gold-encrusted night! All else in the shadows. The Indian playing the harp. The Indians ushering platters in and out. The Indians decanting the wine. The table was a manger, the good news, a friendship. Drink after drink, the captain's pain increased, and maybe that's why he drank so quickly: at the unexpected and unconfessed demise of his friend the bishop. He mumbled the fondest of farewells. He recalled the fallen cleric's archiepiscopal ambitions, his penchant for finery, his pride in his emerald ring, ah, he grew contemplative, the man-at-arms:

"Vanity of vanities, all is vanity, dear Antonio, vain vanity: what good is gold, what good is pride, what good the truncated path to becoming an archbishop, now that there is no glory for him at all, except the weight of this savage earth over his bones, over his crumbled flesh, surrendered in an instant to the worms as a harlot to a band of sailors?"

"None at all, your lordship, none at all. Faced with death, any glory is but a leaf aflutter in the wind: if there is anything that makes us equals as nobles and peasants and saints and sinners and Indians and white men, it is the dance of the Angel of Death."

The captain bowed his head and sighed: perhaps he was weeping, or seeking something on his plate. He perked up or resigned himself. Sometimes there's no difference. He raised his goblet and threw back his head, filling his mouth with wine.

"Cheers, Antonio. Let us toast to the life that is left to us."

"Cheers, captain. May you live a hundred years more."

"You may call me Ignacio while we dine: I shall always be your captain and you my scribe, but over wine and tête-à-têtes, we are friends."

Eye to eye. A bridge erected, vaulting over the feast to connect two men who resembled each other. Antonio was tall and the captain short, but both were stocky. Antonio's neck was squat and the captain's evoked a small giraffe, but both had brown hair. Antonio had an eagle's profile and the captain an anteater's, but both faces were long. The captain seized his left hand with his right and extended it toward Antonio, who clasped it briskly, and there they were, two friends clasping hands, callus against swashbuckling callus.

"Thank you, your grace, for the honor you afford me."

"Be thankful for the honor of being born Biscayne. O my tongue. I miss it so. I no longer know what I do here or why. I languish each day, awaiting the transfer I requested over one year ago. I take little pleasure in this new inheritance, my monkey soldiers, my foolish little Indians. Nothing surprises nor intrigues me."

Tears streaming down his cheeks, the captain dropped Antonio's hands. Hastened his goblet. Carved his meat. He cut a tremendous morsel and opened his mouth so wide that Antonio confirmed he had all his teeth. At the next available opportunity, he'd ask how he managed to keep his dentition so white and intact; now, the captain urgently needed to speak. Antonio glimpsed the full contents of his mouth. The meat more pulverized with every word. A fine mist of pork and wine spraying him.

"Why did I come? There are times when I forget, my dear friend. I wished to see the world, I wished to gather gold, I wished to be a lord, more lordly than I already was, for I was born a nobleman, but a second-born son. My father left me something, though not enough; my lady is also noble, and noble her dowry, but I wished to earn my fortune with my own sword. I left everything behind in Spain in hopes that I might prosper swiftly. Ten years have passed, and I have done it: I have lands and a hacienda, I have rank and office, I have a thousand Indians, I could have tenfold if I wished. But I wish to go home. I could leave my affairs to someone willing to manage them and send me the doubloons. I wish to eat *kokotxas* and *porrusaldas*, toast with *irulegi* and with *calimochos*; I wish to play the *txistu* and the *tamboril*, to dance *aurresku* and burn the *Markitos* at Carnival. And if there is one thing I ask of God, it is to spare me the kind of death inflicted on my poor friend, alas, who perished among savages in this savage land, so far from my people that I would not even perish in my own tongue."

"To die in Biscay: a noble ambition. Ah, but who does not yearn to die at home. Better indeed to drink, eat, and dance at home, you are quite right. To flee before time runs out, return to the motherland—not like the holy bishop, no, poor bishop, oh, how cruel the Angel of Death. I have seen her so many times in my soldiering days. I have dodged her and dealt her. No, not dealt: who can give what is already given? The only certainty of those who are born is that they must die: death is always already given to us. If there is one thing we have done as men-at-arms, it is merely to hasten death, am I right?"

"O you are clever, yes, most excellently clever. You say it is impossible to kill: then I have killed no one. How clever, very clever. Yes, I have simply hastened the death of a few. I am fire that does not burn, a holy assassin. Indeed you are very, very clever. As I am innocent."

"Any instant of human life is a new execution. And thus I am warned how frail life is, how wretched and how vain!"

His superior shed a fat, heavy tear. He was drunk. He clutched his new friend's hands again. And pressed his brow to Antonio's. Acidic, the captain's breath.

"How wise your words and how noble your throat, which proffers truths and sings songs like a little Biscayne girl. Sing me something now."

"I do not sing like a girl, I was only dreaming of the sister I left behind in Spain when she was very small."

"Sing to me like an old man or like a girl or like a goldfinch, as long as you sing in Biscayne, for my ears and my very soul ache from the strain of endless barbarities crowed in Castilian. It pains me more than the savage tongues."

"I will sing you whatever you wish, but let us pray for your friend to be dealt a merciful judgment. ..." Antonio prayed, and the captain closed his eyes. Antonio sprinkled poppy powder into his chalice. If anyone saw, no one cared. The prayer came to an end, *sed libera nos a Malo, amen.* He proposed a toast to the soul of the good bishop. They drained their glasses and Antonio began to sing.

"Andere Santa Klara hantik phartitzen," he continued in his silken tenor's voice, and the captain's face sweetened as he sang along.

"Haren peko zamaria ürhez da zelatzen ..." they sang together, as if rowing, to the same rhythm, the same canoe over the surface of the gentlest river. And they drank. They ran out of wine.

"Ardo gehiago! Ireki beste upel bat!" the captain shouted, utterly bereft of his Castilian. "Ardo gehiago, ergel basatiak!" he boomed to savages too petrified to guess the obvious.

The captain stood. His chair clattered to the ground. He struck the table with both fists. The scraps of his main course leapt into the air. A leg bone. The great head. A section of ribs. Our captain shouted again, steady as in battle. He seized the nearest Indian by the shirt, shook him, howled in his ear. The poor Indian didn't speak Biscayne. The captain crushed him against the wall. Walloped him twice. Spilled him onto the floor.

"Ahizpa, enükezü ez sinhetsia …" Antonio kept singing to the strumming of the harp, ecstatic at the sight of his own reflection gleaming on the silver platter that the captain's thump had borne up to his face. The bronze of the candlestick shimmering across his new doublet, the silken threads of his ruff, the golden hilt of the captain's rapier. He'd grabbed it in the commotion. Gold against gold, this pleased Antonio, maybe he'd make off with the sword when the brute finally succumbed to his slumber. But not yet. The captain wasn't falling. He seized another Indian. Twisted his arm. Dislocated his shoulder. Pushed him down to his knees. The Indian said I do not understand, I do not understand, my lord, forgive me, my lord, I do not understand. He looked up at the captain in a perilous attempt at making himself understood. The wager went poorly.

"How dare you set eyes on me, you insolent Indian!"

The captain's temper kindled like coal. Violet, the veins of his temples. Mouth open. Teeth clenched. Hand ablaze. He grasped his lash and struck the Indian. Lashed and thrashed. Antonio now sang in a little girl's voice, and in Castilian, the song of his Virgin. He didn't think it was right to strike anyone for not being able to speak Biscayne. If it were, then most of Spain, the New World and the Old, and the globe itself would be bruised and battered. The captain felled one man. Then another. And sent yet another to the ground. Then he stopped. And dropped the lash. He looked at Antonio. A sweet and baffled smile. He asked:

"What is the worst of all fates for a shepherd?"

And at last he crumpled, to the relief of each and every Indian. And Antonio, who was weary of singing alone, and of his own reflection. He wanted to decamp and honor his Virgin of the Orange Grove by keeping the promise he'd made to her.

"To count sheep and nod off."

This was his reply to his captain, who was snoring. He picked up the rapier, which hadn't stopped gleaming. And the clinking pouch of coins. The officer would need to sleep for quite a while. Perhaps an entire day. Perhaps a week. Or more. He dragged him to his bower. Left him slumped in it. Kissed him on the forehead. And left with pouch, tapir's leg, and sword in hand.

17

The light barely moves. But it does move. Is anything still except him? Not even him. His hand also moves, back and forth. And he breathes as he writes. He runs and yells when Kuaru and Tekaka or the girls make off with his sword or dagger, giggling as they escape. Antonio didn't know that monkeys laughed until one day they pelted him with pacará pods. Now he knows it, but barely even notices their laughter, as he understands that the breeze rustling the leaves is faint because the light barely moves. The shadows are often softer here in the jungle, which is dense with shade, though it also lives in the light of the sun, like everything else in this world. Like the she-leopard with the luminous aura he sees each night, circling the hut, licking the faces of Mitākuña and Michī, who curl their tiny bodies between the great cat's paws. He wakes every time with his heart thrashing in his chest, fleet and furious. He opens his eyes. Nothing but the girls asleep. And something like fireflies flitting around them. He knows fear, Antonio does. And the she-jaguar terrifies him. It's the jungle itself baring its teeth, showing its strength, its hunger. Its means of giving death. Just like that, in a flash, like a lightning bolt cast down by God. Maybe God is a she-jaguar. Or the beetle he's just spied inside a flower. Like a precious stone glittering in the fragrance of the blossom's white cup. He doesn't know. But what he does know is that he's surrounded by Indians who are looking after him. Why? What has he done for anyone to look after him? It must be a miracle of the Virgin of the Orange Grove. Or else because he's protecting the girls. Another miracle. Like the beetle. The she-jaguar. The river. The smooth black stone under the clear water. Like these girls and these creatures sheltering between his legs, as if his legs could protect them. Maybe they can. Antonio sings. And returns to his letter. Just for the sake of writing, of swaying to his own music, of stopping. Stopping.

I let myself be borne like a feather by the wind; if the muleteer had gone to Rome, then perhaps today I would be pope. Forgive me, dear aunt, I mean no blasphemy, keep reading, I pray and entreat you; I would be a painter of churches or a philologist. I remember little of the journey, except that it was long and arduous. I felt wrested violently from the earth and could not comprehend such abandonment, I who had wished for no roots, having left them with you, in our walnut grove; I left them to your care and to the care of the birds, the sheep, the dogs, and the little milk cow and her calves, and to you, and you too I left to the care of the walnut grove. Perhaps not: I left no one to the care of anyone, I fled for myself, the handsome animal of my body had awakened, wishing to run free as all animals do, and I hadn't regretted it before, nor did I regret it then, I did not wish to return, but I did feel borne like a feather by the wind. I trust you will remember the sort of person that I am, dear aunt, you know there is nothing of the feather in me, I am strong and heavy as my father was, stronger perhaps, for I undertake nearly all of my labors myself, my poor servants are neither mine nor servants, rather I serve them and they are people of meager mettle, yet on my journey I was light and fragile, and I was forced to drift in fear, short of breath and with my throat constrained, as if some fanged and amorphous beast were ever about to swallow me down for breakfast.

"Your angels are spirits, che. Half bird half man."
    "Mba'érepa?"

"Because they have wings, Michī."

"Are there girl angels, che?"

"Angels are neither boys nor girls."

"Like you."

"I am a man, Mitākuña."

"Nde japu."

"I am a woman?"

"Nahániri."

"So what am I, then?"

"Angel, che. Big ugly bird."

The girls giggle. Antonio also laughs: he doesn't need anyone to tell him what he is. And he could do far worse than an angel. He returns to his aunt.

Perhaps it was the land, not merely my father who had overlooked me; how little he knew me, because he barely had a chance to know me; not only did he commend me to your care, yet he wished for you to raise me into a prioress, how could he have ever seen me as a page? He should have seen me as a lieutenant years later and I should have made myself known, yet I refused. There he stayed, in his old Spain, where people are born as what they are meant to be forever, or else they are nothing. However, perhaps it wasn't only this, perhaps it was Castille, Castille the eternally arid, bereft of trees, bereft of roots, although she persists, having been planted there many ages ago, was she not? Is it not true that Castille has always been there ...

"Mitākuña, I have no wings."

"We make them for you. Or you dream."

"If I dream of being a bird, will I fly?"

"If you dream it, che."

"Make me some wings, then, little one."

Calm returned to me, dear aunt, with deep, full breaths, with the air drawn unthinkingly into the lungs, good air, as soon as we crossed the Peaks of Europe, when I first saw the forest blanketing the earth, and I was filled with its damp scent of a well-lived life, its minty pine, its sea lapping at its shores. Yet I was not bound to remain in Bilbao, as I would find no form of employ, nor any dwelling but prison, nor any friends but strangers.

It was thus; I was strolling behind the cathedral, where I had gone to pray to Saint Anthony, whose beautiful chapel is there, and bid him to help me in my plight; poor, how poor I was, and he had bequeathed his money to the poor; I lacked for shelter, and he had dwelled in a cave. And I recalled the tales you always told me, back when I was the apple of your eye, the child at your skirts, your neska: *how once a wild sow had gone to see him, with all her piglets in tow, the very image of the ones we glimpsed in the woods one day when we went foraging for mushrooms with the sisters, just like the piglets we saw, tiny, with large pink snouts and great dark eyes and diminutive pink lashes and black spots, and stripes up and down their brown hide, just as beautiful as that, you told me, but her piglets were born blind. The wild sow bowed before the saint, and the saint saw the supplication in her reverence, and he also saw the little piglets lurching and colliding with things and falling and struggling up again. He took pity and cured them with his holy hand. And the sow and her piglets loved him forever and always protected him from vermin and from men. Only from the devil did they fail to protect him, though the saint himself could do so, you told me, but you didn't tell me the entire story, the temptations, each assuming the form of a maid more tempting than the last, not to mention the occasional lad. No indeed, the devil spared him nothing, poor Anthony.*

"Hey, che, what color for your wings?
  "Any color you like."

"Red and black?"

"Mba'érepa?"

"Like Satan?"

"Yes."

"Why?"

"So you can make fire, che."

"Better make them white or blue or green or orange."

"Mba'érepa?"

"I can make fire without being a demon, Michī."

But oh, my aunt, again my memory leads me about at whim; just now it led me back to your skirts, to the tender tales you told me when I was very small, and here I was telling you how I found myself in prison for the first time. Other times followed. Many others, pour yourself another cup, eat a pintxo *or two, and then, if you wish, keep reading these words. I was walking as I pondered where to sleep that night, and the answer appeared in the form of three young boys who surrounded me and began to insult me. That I was dressed like a Moor, had a nose like a Jew, small hands like a fairy, a buggerer, begging for a beating, and right then and there one gave me a shove and I fell to the ground, and this fall was in fact a stroke of luck, because beside my hand was a stone. I was able to stand, I don't remember how, just as I don't remember how I succeeded in splitting one of their heads, which thumped on the ground like a tangerine, brains scattering about. And the two sounds: the stone striking the skull and echoing through my body, then the man striking the earth. Both sounds pleased me, as did the newborn might of my hand that could strum them like a lute, but then my fortune ran out; as if by magic, two sentries appeared and seized me. I slept that night, relieved of wondering where I would find a bed, yet weighing whether I could afford to spend more money on inns and to depart that city as swiftly as I could. Yet Bilbao did not love me; the man who had dishonored and attacked me took a full month to heal. A gentleman cannot brook such affronts; to be a man means to defend his honor to the death, his own death if necessary; to uphold the honor, let me explain, that upholds him in turn. Others must see his readiness to kill so that he may live, although this end, the ability to live, may cost a man his life. Have I made myself clear, dear aunt? Like the all-too-heavy pack that one must sometimes carry for the sake of food and shelter and money on the road, for arduous and often deadly are the roads when one has neither pack nor money.*

Honor costs life or lives, like a horse with a taste for human flesh, and you must relinquish a phalanx or an entire finger if you wish to travel far. I don't know if I have made myself understood, yet this is how it comes to me now; I don't know if I could suffer my honor to be lost, if I could permit myself such a thing, not even now that I am, as I have said, a man of peace, a muleteer. I could not brook it; should my honor be stolen, I would be made a servant or a corpse. There is no other way to be a man, a free man. One must kill if necessary. I have slain many, many more than necessary, will you forgive me for it? I still bear my knife and sword, my harquebus and powder.

The horses haven't come back.

18

"Valiant soldiers, Christian soldiers of valorous Spain! Our magnanimous captain commands we drink to the eternal rest of the holy bishop. Open ten barrels of wine posthaste and pray till dawn for his good soul."

He'd chosen a mare and moved in the shadows, just in case. But what case? If wine has the force of a waterfall. Wine forges paths where there are none. Wine always finds a way. Like a branch whisked along the rapids, so did wine convey him. What a curious thing, this wine that led him west and dragged the soldiers east. The sharpest among them had their suspicions, since the captain had never before been so generous, but all it took was a swig of Rioja to rouse them. To the shout of carpe diem, God keep our holy bishop in his glory, viva, hurrah, they left the guard posts, the beds, the prayers, and the orgies behind. They craved good wine in their mouths more than they craved going home. More than a woman. After nightfall, even more than gold. And night had fallen indeed. The poor Spanish poor were sick of swallowing the spit of foul-breathed Indians. And the New World–born criollos longed to wreathe their throats in the silk of Castille, which, they were convinced, would make them more Spanish than their uniforms could, or the names of the ships on which their fathers or grandfathers had sailed. They drink chicha when they have no choice, but it's wine they want, and Spanish wine at that. As God wills: it's either the blood of Christ or a good Rioja, they sang, buoyant. Swiftly they opened barrels and brought glasses, or coconut halves, and threw themselves under the scarlet stream, dazed and delighted. Wine from Spain, ay, thank you, sweet Jesus, dear Father, receive the good bishop in Your glory. Swiftly, too, proceeded Antonio to the captain's office. He unlatched the monkeys' cage; he hadn't promised this to his Virgin, but he opened it. The monkeys didn't move. They were indifferent to everything, could endure no more. Antonio lowered the tapestry bearing the coat of arms from the wall and swaddled them. To open the girl's cage, which was locked tight, he used his cutlass. The girl was huddled in the farthest corner of the cage. Terrified. Afraid to emerge. She feared the man, who forced half his towering body inside and dragged her out. She smelled bad and was cold to the touch. He opened his shirt and brought her to his skin. Wrapped her in the captain's cape. Picked up the bundle of monkeys. Crept soundless in the dark to the mare awaiting him, saddled and laden with provisions. He was startled to find a colt beside the mare. Two horses, then: that's good. He walked slowly. Led them by the reins. He didn't want to be heard. The others would be glad to have one less mouth swilling the wine that now belonged to all of them. But how to be sure? There are always risks. Some embittered abstainer. Or an ambitious sort more covetous of honors than of wine. He left slowly. Drifted away from the bellowing soldiers.

Silent, he delved deeper into the jungle. He didn't know where he was going, how far he'd get on this journey. He could hear his own body and the body of the Indian girl. Her delicate breath against his flesh, his chest splitting. Something crept into his throat and clutched at him. *Madre mía.* He hugged the sorrel, taking care not to suffocate the child. He had to dismount. The jungle is intricate, he saw only green, the same tissue everywhere. He couldn't take the usual path. Or maybe he could. He could take it and gallop, get as far as possible. A sky riddled with stars was his witness. And the vulture, stirring. It swiveled the rough hide of its head. Beheld them with one eye. Then the other. Barely a rustle to acknowledge their leaving. Kept sleeping. There was a long stretch of darkness still. A howl. A young dog. Not many dogs around here. Antonio likes them. He stopped, searched, and found it. A little coppery dog, Red, Antonio named her. She wagged her tail. In a thicket of climbing plants and ferns, beside her, another gaunt and tiny child. Asleep. Or unconscious. She didn't wake, didn't react. Maybe she'd be thirsty, too. He hoisted both girls onto the horse, bound them to his body with the captain's cape. Two monkeys, two girls, one dog, two horses. He'd better hurry. Gallop. The dull blow of horseshoes on earth. Branches slashing at his skin. He didn't want to be too late. How late was too late? It could be too late right now! Perfect is the enemy of good. While he'd promised oranges, they wouldn't be able to eat unless they survived. Better to give them water. He decided to stop. He sat on the root of a tall tree. He opened the cape and gave them water from his canteen. The eldest twitched, drank, then vomited. Slower, then. A round of little sips. The monkeys, too; they perked up a bit and clutched each other tighter. Some water for Red as well. The younger child curled her hand around his finger. And then Antonio knew. He heard the singing in his head: the angelic choir that sang to him earlier, not long ago at all, about the Virgin and the orange grove. His deeds were pleasing to his Virgin and also to the holy child, to her and to Him. He gave them bread soaked in water. He tucked both girls back under his shirt, against his skin, secured with the cape.

"Thank you, che, señor."

The eldest said it. Antonio didn't answer, just hugged his cargo and stroked his garment in a single proud gesture. Something swelled in his chest. Now he wouldn't have to stop until he reached the orange grove, if there was in fact an orange grove.

And if not, he'd stop under some banana trees. Or some palm trees. Or trees bearing some kind of fruit. As long as they were far from the captain, who would wake within hours. Days at most. He wasn't coming back. Time to run. The cruel soldier was soon to rouse. And in a mood most foul, this much was certain.

19

That first day in the jungle, the day he fled, he still didn't know how to see. Now he does. It's nearly impossible in this world of plants. But he sees it. A tender vine shoot veers around itself until it meets another, intertwining myriad. Like droplets in the rivers they wet. They shift and shift together into oneness, then send out another shoot as green and strong and delicate as the first, which joins it. The jungle's green is made of animals that grow a new foot for every step they take. That's how it is, he's seeing it at last, the world expanding inward. He's already roamed far and wide. On land and over mountains. On seas and savannas. In battles and halls. And now it happens that he can burrow deep into each expanding interior.

The day's sweet warmth caresses his tribe. His animals and his children in the grace of the sun. Antonio feels good. He likes to watch them shine this way, softly, in peace, nestled against him in this land of trunks and roots and vines and leaves and leaves and leaves. They're in the weave of the jungle. He smiles. He could spend the rest of his life like this, he thinks. A damp heat suddenly bathes his belly. A stench blots his smile. What could it be? Yes: the girls. Oh God. The brown smear spreads across his garments. To the river, then. He's grateful to the Lord for providing the jungle with so much water. And grateful that he thought to grab two extra shirts and pairs of breeches. And the beautiful tapestry that has served as a sheet for them. They must have done it on purpose. They don't want to go back, he concludes. Which is only reasonable. What other weapons might these tiny creatures brandish? Could such a deed be done deliberately? Fear overtakes him when he considers the imperial coat of arms, formerly gold. These Indians respect nothing. Not even when one saves their lives and lets them eat. And drink. How dare they. The coat of arms. What could be next? The cross? Does he even have a cross? The gold one he wore around his neck, a gift from his aunt—he lost it at cards. These girls. Michī and Mitākuña. He's kept his promise to the Virgin of the Orange Grove. He could leave them here. The choir is still nearby. They'd come to their aid. They're already feeding them. If they didn't, he'd be abandoning the pair to their death. Perhaps that's their fate. Perhaps he's only delaying it. Perhaps he ought to abandon them as a fallen trunk is left to be swept away by the river. He'd move faster without them. But where? Where could he reinvent himself this time? Another name. A new livelihood. He could return to Spain. No one wants to kill him there, although he'd have to die regardless. Of boredom. Of being himself forever. The repugnant smell and, worse, the feel. Now begins the delicate task of opening his shift. Removing the rest of his clothes. Taking a length of linen. A bar of soap. Picking up the girls. Walking to the river. Lowering them into the water. Bathing them. Bathing himself. Setting them in the light. Plunging his garments into the river, and the emblem of the empire on which the sun will never set again, oh, Mitākuña and Michī, for the water to cleanse the filth. And he leaves them as free of consequences as he imagines the sky over the Sphinx, arid and luminous. Getting his clothes. Dressing himself. Then vomiting, yes. He is astonished by his innards. Shrewdly they'd waited for him to resolve all urgent matters before stampeding, charging out of him and hurling their contents to the ground like monkeys. Where are the monkeys. He leans against a tree. Looks up. He sees they're wet. They must have bathed themselves. They're lying belly-up on the branches of a tree so beautiful it could be a thing of Satan. Antonio has gone to the river every day. He doesn't know how he never noticed this beast of many boughs skewed in all directions, yet crowned by a single lush canopy. The trunks and branches, almost entirely obscured by leaves, venture occasional glimpses of soft, cinnamon-hued bark. Pale spots here and there. Festooned with fruits. The small ones are green; the medium-sized, red; the largest, black. Glossy and round as enormous grapes. Gleaming fruits. Full. Burnished as the captain's bald spot beneath the futile trick of combing over the scant hair at his nape. Fruits glittering as the obsidian eyes of melted Indians. Splendid fruits coat the trunk from the ground up. The monkeys reach out and stuff their mouths with them.

"My macaques, have you found the orange grove in these jungles? Do you think it will please the Virgin? And the girls?"

He walks to the tree. Lets himself be embraced by the monkeys, who scale his legs. He plucks a fruit and bites it. Paradise. If Paradise is real—not even as a novice was he sure—it must be something like this. The rupture of the sweet fruit in his mouth. The miracle that enthralls his tongue. The sun on his skin. His body in the water. Paradise is made of such things. And nothing more, nothing at all: this great jet-skinned grape, its white, luscious flesh and two violet pits, does away with all ills, even bad memories. And bad smells. Antonio picks more grapes and returns to the girls. Sits down on the cloth. Splits the fruits. He removes the pits and skin and presents them to the children. Mitākuña chews slowly. Michī doesn't want to eat. Antonio, reduced to a big ugly bird once more, chews a bit himself and puts it into her mouth. Michī swallows. He does this several times. Until she turns her face away. Enough. The girls are still. Content with the taste of the fruit in their mouths, perhaps. Or with the bud of a newborn silk floss leaf. It opens like a balled fist. They all look in the same direction. Antonio has been writing with such furor that he's barely noticed anything else. The jungle is a colossus weaving itself together. But only this did he notice. He didn't even realize that his shirt was scratching at his chest. He stops, unbuttons it. And regards himself. Two round and tender pellets. Two baby blossoms on his old scarred skin. Nipples. Pink and smooth. He's always had them. But it's today that he feels them ache against the weave of his shirt.

"Hey, che, we are going."
   "Going where?"
   "To find your feathers."
   "Sing as you go. So I can hear you."

When the door of my prison in Bilbao swung open, that is when I began to travel far, dear aunt. In one way or another I had remained close by; at such a distance that I could return to you by donkey or on foot if necessary. I began to take my definitive leave with no clear destination, yet first I resolved to visit Donostia, and our convent, arriving most handsome and composed, having secured worthy garments and tolerable shelter. It was thus that I walked like a soldier for the first time; with martial resolution, with my eyes in plain sight, I made my way to the convent. I attended the entire mass. I wished my neighbors peace. My mother saw me and kissed me, but she did not recognize me. Not a glance from my father. I don't know, and may never know, if you recognized me. I think you did; your eyes met mine. I trembled, my dear, perhaps with fear, perhaps with longing for you to notice me. You lowered your gaze and kept singing—did you set me free? Or forget me altogether? Impossible. Perhaps you didn't know that it was me; you too were only able to imagine me as a maid. I have said I left without bidding you farewell, which is not entirely the truth, what else did it mean for me to go to mass, what else but to bid you farewell. To you and to Spain itself. I left like someone who rushes into the greatest of battles, but knows nothing of war; with his spirits high, with the light heart of a little bird setting off on its first great migration. I made arrangements with a sailor and set off for Seville, magnificent Seville. There, despite an invitation to stay, I left for Sanlúcar. An uncle of mine took me on as a cabin boy. Oh, beloved aunt, the vast horizon of the sea! The endless sky reflecting it, the mermaids, the rough labors of men. I left, I came.

20

He sailed the river's skin in his skin, by night, when even the vultures sleep. Floating on his back in warm waters. The captain was losing rank and insignias. He surrendered to a tender current. Yacaré yrupés level with his benevolently weeping eyes. Flowers. He saw the fat petals rising redly from the green centers of the platter-like lily pad of the yrupé. He saw them warping into arches, opening, then closing tight into white tips. They did not appear to him as complete forms; they were happening, right now. In every petal, the vegetal milk, condensed into small reddish orbs, spread its arms to converge with the others. They reached and stretched. They grew paler the more they knotted and drifted from the base. They all vibrated like small animals, delighted to be brushing up against each other. Sheer shaded restlessness, this flower, said to himself the one who was not, just then, a captain. He too was a yrupé. His abdomen a blossoming green plate, pink flower with a heart of yarn, heads bathed in greasy golden dust. It grew in him and thrummed. The captain hummed a skirmish. Hummed a skin in his skin. Hands in his hands. Eyes in his eyes. He hummed, most of all, a voice in his ears, in his stomach, a voice caressing his intestines before emerging with its face turned sunward, the flower of his secret flowering there. He hummed, lulled by the angelic voice of a girl who made him strain toward the light. It made him pulse yacaré yrupé. Yacaré, toothed flower, he thought, these fucking Indians are mad. He laughed and shifted his head. Poor captain, the yacaré lost all its yrupé, bit his neck from within, and then there was neither river nor flower. There was nothing but the caiman biting him and the clay banks of these repugnant rivers. The sharp, rank current brimmed in his throat, rising from his belly. Or from a shit-filled hell, he wasn't sure, and he didn't care who was ravaging his innards. He opened his eyes and the volcano of his guts engulfed them at once. He couldn't even close his mouth. Or speak. Couldn't call for help. Or move his head. Barely his hands. Each tiny movement unleashed a foul torrent that warmed his chest, only to cool it down again, and a herd of yacarés multiplied, gnawing at the back of his head. He had to stay still. Breathe slowly. Someone would come to his aid. He studied the ceiling: the palm fronds mixed with mud, the insect nests. He couldn't understand where his Indians had gone. Or his soldiers. Or his secretary. He saw it was day. Water, he said. Water.

"Go fuck yourself, che, señor."

The voice belonged to an Indian. He said something else in his own tongue. The captain recognized it. Inferred a new insult. He was startled. More startling were the two hands that clutched his neck. If he hadn't needed to devote the whole of his energy to shaking them off, he would have sunk into a motionless perplexity.

"Hey, che. Die now, chief, die."

The Indian's sentence was highly descriptive. If he failed to wrest those hands from his neck within a minute, the captain would give up the ghost. He didn't hear the sound of the blow that released him, but he exhaled with such force and relief that he decided he would dedicate the rest of his life to it. To breathing, that is. He opened his eyes. He saw a soldier with high cheekbones and a cat's eyes. He assumed he was hallucinating and fainted again. We don't know if he heard the soldier:

"Fucking brutes. You civilize 'em, teach 'em to wipe their ass, then they stab you in the back first chance they get. May as well kill 'em all."

21

He slept like a log, not that his sleep was profound. Or long. He slept like a log because he was enlaced with the tiny arms and legs of the two monkeys and the two girls and Red's small head. He feels the warmth of their skin. Their diminutive breaths. Antonio is a tree. And boughs his troops. He'll be sprouting leaves and casting shade any minute now. Well, he already casts shade. And sees in green. With one light slap, he parts the tender vegetal warp the jungle has blanketed them with, slipping into the hut. Soon the sun will set. The insect clouds are fierce. The jaguar roars. The flowers close. Yellow eyes flash in the dark: fireflies. What do fireflies capture in their nighttime raids? They drink, they must drink water like all other animals, even the trees. Except for men, who drink water as well, but also wine and liquor and moonshine and chicha. Other creatures drink other things. Mosquitoes, for instance, now darting gregariously about, with their air of large predators. He'd better light the fire again, it's nearly out. He moves very slowly. Peels arms and legs from his trunk. He settles the girls into the shape of a nut: Mitākuña and Michī are the seed, Kuaru and Tekaka the protective shell. He covers them with his cape. It's always winter for the weak. He was never so cold as when he couldn't even stand, had crumpled to the ground. Or maybe that wasn't weakness. It could have been the weather in the mountains up above. Or both. He likes to see them like this, peaceful. Michī opens her eyes, enormous in a face no longer so gaunt—how has this happened so quickly? Her cheeks have filled out. She stares at Antonio, who feels those eyes on him. He bears them like newborn fruit. It's a lot of work to be a tree. He'd never thought of it before. Even stones work. He writes.

My hands were flayed as I raised and lowered sails, dear aunt, tied knots and untied them, clung to or fled from things set loose when the sea blustered. Harsh is the labor of a sailor. Fortune willed us south, into the heat, into the sun that cracked the skin, at midday, along the Guadalquivir, which is a river; I made my debut in gentle waters. We saw San Juan de Aznalfarache, then a great city governed by Moors, the two great pilasters that were all that was left of its bridge; only the men who hail from here can traverse this river without sending their ships straight into them and running aground in the shallows. We reached the key of Sanlúcar, where one emerges onto the Ocean Sea and loses the scent of sweetness, where all is saltpeter and fish, even the men. Spain began to shrink, behind, behind, until the horizon folded and there was nothing but the sea itself in all directions. Yet it is not empty; we were followed by hundreds of enormous fishes with dread teeth, a cabin boy fell in, we flung the rowboat overboard and he was devoured before it met the water. In moments, a man became a paltry red stain, then nothing; one swore he saw the largest shark spitting out a femur like a toothpick. I did not see it. Flying fishes also came after us, my dear, spearing the air like silver arrows, so many all together that they resembled an island. And birds surrounded us. Rarely could I stop to behold such marvels, busy as I was bandaging my hands, which stung all day long, and devoting myself to my new duties. I could tell you however of the storms, how the entire world became a squall and the waves devour you and there is neither above nor below but simply a clutching to something and spinning about, a colliding into everything, a shattering into a thousand pieces and praying for it to clear. We were consoled by Saint Elmo when he appeared shining like a torch, like a lantern on our vessels in the

darkest night. He accompanied us for two hours and some were
blinded when he had gone. I retained my sight, my dear, and could
even see how the stars wheeled overhead, how we lost the north star
as our guide and new ones appeared. By the time we arrived, the sun
had weathered my skin and chapped it, yet my hands were callused
at last. I was ready, aunt, for I did not know what awaited me.

"Hey, che, lie down, Antonio."
  "Why?"
  "Because now you have your wings."
  "May I see before you put them on me?"
  "Nahániri."

22

He, Ignacio, has made it to the other side. He recognizes his bed with its Granadan canopy. His sheets, his family crest. His Biscayne tapestry of ships, fishermen, the Donostian sea and sky. And the gloom of his chambers pierced by a ray of sunlight, then dulled in turn by the drapery, that enters only to silhouette his greenish face, his gleaming pate, his hands resting on his belly, against the dark background. He woke hours ago, but his head impedes him from sitting. It weighs too much, charged with intense and lacerating pain. He thinks it must be God's rage lancing a thousand lightning bolts into his skull. And his stomach shudders like a thunder-pregnant cloud in the same black stormy sky. His whole body is captive to a squall that knows no mercy. What rage, what God. He wonders if he can feign unconsciousness for one day more. Wonders how many days he's been poisoned. Who knows why he wants to feign. The tooth puller who passes for his physician told him wine was the culprit, but the man's a quack. An Indian witch doctor dancing naked to summon his vulture-faced tree gods has more science than this charlatan. He has been, Ignacio is sure of it, mildly poisoned. He shudders with a stab of ire. He vomits. Brown hands appear in his halo of light. His Indians. He is terrified of them. He howls.

"Not a problem, captain. The guy who nabbed you, plus and his folks and friends and the relatives of his friends and their chickens and their lettuce and all the rest, they're out, I got 'em all for you. These guys right here are good though, more pious than a priest, rest easy. Now look, look at me, and do as I do: first have some tea, breathe in, breathe out."

The head of the catlike soldier enters the beam of light, illuminated, cup in hand. The captain drinks the tea, it does him good. He mimes him, inhales, exhales. What a fine idea, breathing. Yes, he's going to devote himself to this. He does. He inhales. Now, the Indians flitting about leave him nearly as indifferent as ever. Exhales. Looks at them. One bears a cloth to clean the floor. Inhales. Another extends a chalice of water and a pitcher. Another offers him the basin. Exhales. They all seem to materialize from nothing as they approach, emerging from a backdrop of shadows. He must light his chambers properly. If he hadn't tripped a thousand times over different objects on the darkest nights, inhales, he'd swear that only what is in the light exists. In fact, in Castilian, one says "alumbramiento" and "dar a luz" to mean bring forth, give birth, deliver. Delivered unto the light. But the dark is alive, so full of life. Full of Indians. Exhales. The water, clean and wild, rinses his mouth, and when he spits, he likewise spits out fear and fury. He feels touched now, softened. He could be dead instead of mildly poisoned. Inhales. Antonio wanted to put him to sleep, not put him to death. Well, hasten his death. How clever. He thinks he remembers him singing. In a girl's voice. Exhales. Antonio's ugly face looming over his. Shadows swelling until they swallowed him whole, and in the dimmest moment, the surprise of damp lips on his brow. Inhales. Like the graze of one of those plants that thrives in water, the kiss plant, they call it. A reed, a water hyacinth, a yrupé. And a tense smoothness stirring without decorum. Inhales. But whose smoothness. Whose tension. And what modesty. Exhales. Water, he says, and the hands appear once more. He doesn't start. He feels Gato breathing nearby. And proceeds. Inhales. What he needs, he thinks, are some machine hands, bodiless, headless, maybe footed, to serve him. And another machine with nothing but a head to remember what had tormented him mere days before. Exhales. A lifetime ago. The matter of how many postmortem ascensions. He leaves it for later. He drinks, drinks deeply. And decides to permit himself a nap. Inhales. And then who knows. His reverie embraces him.

23

Mitãkuña and Michĩ dance in their sleep. Lulled by the singing of their fellows. Their mothers, their grandmothers must be among the singers. They shift their heads and hum, seemingly sustained by the infinite song that, like days, like nights, neither begins nor ends anywhere at all. It just continues forever. Once again they tell Antonio to lie down on his belly and undress. They only let him keep his underclothes. Antonio's skin looks like a map. Furrowed with rivers, mountains, ravines. The girls have woven feathers from a net of vegetal threads. A great long hexagon across his back, a compact band bound around his torso: to the tattered leather, utter scars, a single flap and two nipples that Antonio has for a chest. The feathers that form the base of the wings are a dark and brilliant blue. They're from a smooth-billed ani bird. Above, all hues of them. Green, red, turquoise, orange, yellow, purple.

"Hey, che, stand up."

"Mba'érepa?"

"To see him be a bird, Michĩ."

"Here I am, little ones."

"Good, che."

"Guyra ivaietereíva."

"No, Michĩ, he is not ivaietereíva, not an ugly bird, he is pretty, porã, che."

"Ivaietereíva."

"Iporã."

"Ivaietereíva."

"Iporã."

"Ivaietereíva."

"Iporã."

"Stop shouting, you imps."

"Fly, che."

"No."

"Hey, che, climb a tree."

"Mba'érepa?"

"He is a bird-man-woman, che."

"Héẽ."

"Climb."

Antonio obeys. He makes his way up the thick stalks of the vines that hug the yvyrá pytá tree. The roots and leaves of the güembé plants crown him once he's reached the foliage. The girls stand below, two steps from the hut. They crane their little necks. Antonio looks to be on the brink of flight. The wings spread beyond him, radiant, dark, speckled with color. The tender nipples on his rough torso, crossed by the feathered band. Short legs. Feet clutching the branch like claws. Hooked nose. A warrior bird who's survived the war. The girls lower their heads to glance at each other. They resume their argument.

"Ivaietereíva."

"Iporã."

"Quiet, you two."

"Sing, big bird."

Antonio sings the song about the Virgin of the Orange Grove. He sings it in his girl voice. Their eyes fix on him like fruits again. He's a bird. A bird with four fruits. He's a warrior. A girl among girls. Mitãkuña knows the song. They sing it together several times. Rehearse some variations. They lace their voices together as the güembé wreathes a trunk. As the voice of the yacutinga bird caresses the stream. Kuaru and Tekaka climb up to join him. They sway to the melody, backs turned, tails interwoven. Red softly howls. Antonio grows tired. Asks permission to descend. They grant it. Ceremoniously they remove his wings. They warn the monkeys and Red not to touch them, then step into the brush to search for things. They don't say what.

"Sing as you go. I wish to hear you."

It is done, my aunt. I told you the first of my crimes and I shall continue, I swear. I shall set down the full report, which is nearly the same as telling you the story of my life; I won't exclude a single Indian, a single animal, a single Spaniard, a single tree. I lie, my beloved; a man cannot spend his whole life writing, he must seek sustenance. It is written; the proverbial sweat of the brow, which sweats, here, even if you keep as still as stone. Yet stones need not move, for other stones sustain them. All other things move and restore them, motionless, into the hot and tumultuous heart of the earth, to crackle until they melt and burble, and are heaved up so they can go still once more in cold solidity and then split open and so forth. No, dear aunt, I don't know what this whole bit about the stones amounts to. I must be going in circles to avoid the inevitable; that is, my full confession. Would you be a witness in my favor before the judgment of the Lord? Wait, do not yet answer me.

First, I wish to tell you where I am writing from; from this jungle, which is, for me, a kind of waiting. I am waiting, aunt. To emerge alive, of course, yet bound for where, and for what purpose. This jungle is immense, a world inside the world. Full of water; it rains and rains and also makes me drip, and makes the plants and animals drip, and one could say that all these drops join those of the rivers, the streams, the ponds large and small, and evaporate, only to fall on us once more. I am sitting at the edge of water, a lake perhaps, amid the foliage of some bristly trees, on earth that, curiously, is not red. For the earth is red in this jungle, or else it is

*made of black rocks, enormous and soft. Yet not here. I am still,
like a stone myself, away from my girls, the monkeys, and Red the
dog. I had two horses, but they have been gone for days. Servants, I
have none, and if I am indeed a muleteer, it is for these girls. They
are my cargo. I have lied to you a bit, I know, and so I implore
your forgiveness; all things happen so quickly, and falsehoods have
become something of a custom for me over these furious years. I lie,
beloved, so that I might live. Just slightly more often than most,
who seldom change their names. Yet I am confessing to you now. I
look after them, the Indian girls, for I made a promise to the Virgin
of the Orange Grove, the one from the carol: "Oh blind man, tell
me, blind man, would you an orange give." And the nearby Indians
look after me, you ought to hear them, singing all day like cicadas. If
cicadas sang like angels, perhaps they would be angels. Or Indians.
We are surrounded by them, their voices reach us from the north
and south, from the east and west and everywhere in between. They
send us food, most delicious food. I promised the Virgin I would
return the girls to the Indians alive. I know not why their fellows
do not come for them, why they only stay close by and sing, why
they make this jungle pulse with an air of paradise, if paradise had
any life beyond His own.*

*The girls are two, dear aunt. They are very small. One, the
littlest, Michī is her name, has only grown her first milk teeth, and
the eldest, Mitākuña, has but a few of the new ones, and gaps in her
smile, which is splendid, dear aunt, like the earliest beams when the
sky clears after a storm over the open sea, like finding pure water
in the desert, like a lullaby sung by your mother, or your aunt, my
dearest, when you fear the dark as a child. One talks all day, and
the other has two words at most; she asks why everything is so and
says no to everything as well. Today she spoke a new word in her
savage tongue: ugly, referring to me, as you must have guessed. I
felt the call of the Lady as soon as I saw them; I knew it was She,*

although there were neither lights nor extraordinary fragrances. Yet I knew. I had to help them drink. One was kept prisoner by the captain, I shall tell you about him. I played a trick or two to free her and the monkeys, which were kept in another cage and had no part in my promise to the Virgin; however, disposed as I was to open cages, I went on, I could not restrain myself.

"Girls! Girls! I cannot hear you!"
"We are near, che, do not shout."

I am not a man of admirable restraint, as you shall see. And here we are. I am, as I was saying, at the edge of this water, beneath these leaves, on this pale brown earth infested with insects that luxuriate in nibbling my flesh. A man needs to be alone sometimes. And one who has always been alone, save when he was not a man, at your skirts, needs this like air. I have heard the wingbeat of a humming-bird, oh, dear aunt, if only you could see it, imagine a tiny heart the hue of night, beating swift and incessant, bedecked in rainbow; perhaps you shall glimpse but a shade of this small miraculous bird that relishes sipping from flowers, its tremulous shining restlessness. I have seen the blue gleam of a great ani bird gliding over the water. I have felt how a magpie quivered the hot air with its wings, how it spoke, how the rest of the jungle understood its warning and the monkeys clambered into the heights, and the other birds flew into the distance, and the rodents sank into the depths. A snake must be near. Or a jaguar. I keep still. I smell the intoxicating perfume of a silk floss tree. The urine that I myself have spilled, and which now teems with black butterflies and blue ones, radiant blue like the Mediterranean, and orange and pink ones, and other strange butterflies with the number 88 sketched on the back of their wings; the part you can see when they are folded, dear aunt. For they open and close their wings as if they pulsed. I have also seen a cloud of insects that take pleasure in floating on the water. I observed them for so long, my dearest, that I discovered they do not get wet. Yes, they spend all day falling onto the water, not into it, then taking flight again, seeking or finding who knows what, and no, they don't get wet. They skate over the surface. And whenever they set down their tiny feet, the imperceptible blow sends circles out. Perfect circles that multiply into larger and larger circles, until they vanish. And they do not collide with the circles formed by other insects, as if each occurred on an entirely different layer of the water, and as if the water had hundreds, even thousands of such layers. It must be so, I can see them. I keep still, beloved aunt, as still as I can remember since the day I fled from your side. And perhaps I never kept so still, for before that day I was impelled to seek shelter in you, and then to seek the door leading away from your shelter. I am still as never before. And it is from within this stillness that I am capable of confession, of bearing the weight it takes to be both the impact and the center of the circles, numberless, around it. They arrange themselves around me and I can name them for you. I can tell you, for instance, that the girls weigh on me. Yet they are lovely; their small hands, the way the littlest clutches my fingers, her thick soft hair, her eyes with all their glimmers, the way she speaks to me and the eldest speaks to me. Their smiles, aunt, their pink puppy tongues. They weigh on me, the girls; I owe this stillness to them, this slowness, these hours eager for nothing but writing to you, scratching myself, or eating. I am off to eat, now, for I can smell the food from the Indians on the fire. And I must watch over my girls. My anchors. Could it be that the Virgin wished to give me roots, dear aunt, and earth?

24

He must gather his strength to face the day, to recover his authority. Among such beasts, there's just one way. He must teach them a lesson they'll never forget. Lord. He breathes out: O Lord, the ceremonies. Breathes in. O Lord, the drums of the gallows. Breathes out. O Lord, the ramrod posture. Breathes in. O, the firmness of his command. Breathes out. He'd rather sleep all day. Breathes in. He's still in bed. Better to sleep it off. Gato pours him more tea. Spoons mush into his mouth. Tells him to rest. He breathes in. Gato is good for hangovers. He names him adjutant second lieutenant: his secretary. Orders the appropriate garments to be fetched. He rolls over to face the wall. Breathes out and falls asleep again. Second Lieutenant Gato receives his new rank exultantly. He summons the troops. Explains the captain's situation. Promises them he'll seek the captain's clemency toward the grave offenses committed. Orders them out in platoons to search for gold. If there's no gold, then deliver the Indians who have it. And prepare the ten racks if they refuse to speak. The platoons depart. Second Lieutenant Gato tenderly nurses the captain, reads to him from the book that's all the rage in Spain. It makes Gato laugh. The captain too.

He asked if he had any money; Don Quixote replied that he did not have a copper blanca, *because he never had read in the histories of knights errant that any of them ever carried money. To this the innkeeper replied that he was deceived, for if this was not written in the histories, it was because it had not seemed necessary to the authors to write down something as obvious and necessary as*

carrying money and clean shirts, and if they had not, this was no
reason to think the knights did not carry them ...

"Go on, good Gato, go on reading."

Gato cackles, and so does the captain, who loses control and wets himself. Signaled by Gato, three Indian women tend to the officer's immodesties. The captain appreciates the gesture, feigns ignorance of what's befallen him. This life is good, thinks the captain, touched by a sweetness in the eyes he'd found cunning just hours before. Go on, do go on, and he sips his tea. He nods off again, wet with laughter once more. Gato departs to inspect his troops.

25

Over the river, the moon illuminates a hollow of sky now swooning with orange. Oranges. He couldn't find any oranges for the Virgin. But with this sky and the other fruits brought by Kuaru and Tekaka, he thinks his promise has been kept. The girls sing and the monkeys shimmy into the palms. They've nabbed Antonio's quill. Mitākuña and Michī laugh, Antonio shouts.

"Come down, cursèd simians, come down this instant. If you harm my quill, I will cut off your heads and chew on your brains. Come down!"

Michī touches his leg. Antonio follows her tiny hand with his eyes. She's right: he could offer the monkeys some pindó fruit. He cuts down a bunch with the captain's sword. Tosses a few up to them. They release his quill. He nearly flies, Antonio, darting forth among the vines. He manages to catch the leisurely feather as it flits its way down, bumping through the thickets. The girls keep singing. Kuaru and Tekaka descend. With a sign from Mitākuña, they all sit around the fire. Antonio too.

"Hey, che, listen to our singing."

"Please, go on."

> *Our mama the first mama*
> *made for her body*
> *in the dark before*
> *her legs and feet,*
> *in the dark before before*
> *the very first legs*
> *the very first feet.*

In the dark before
yvoty morotĩ flowers and feathers
grew from her braids
drops of before dew
drops of dew before
before of dew of dew.

In the yvoty morotĩ
of the feather decoration,
the thunder-lightning birdie
mainumby hummingbird
before before mainumby hummingbird
flies flies and flutters
before before with droplets
of dew before
mainumby hummingbird flutters
before before.

As our mama the first mama
wove her own body,
a first wind blew before
before through the droplets.
From the first droplets
came the thunder-lightning birdie mainumby hummingbird.
Before he made
his little house
before he invented
the big blue sky
mainumby hummingbird gave mama water
to drink from his little beak
and the mburukuja of paradise
of the thunder-lightning birdie hummingbird

before before
gave our first mama water
right into her mouth.

Before before
the pindós of paradise
gave our first mama water
before before
the thunder-lightning birdie mainumby
before before
gave our first mama yvoty morotĩ
right into her mouth
before before
sweet yvotyños of paradise
for our mama the first mama,
before before,
the thunder-lightning birdie mainumby hummingbird.

"Nahániri!"
  "Yes, che, Michĩ."
  "Nahániri! Ñanderu."
  "No. Not papa. Mama, Ñandesy."
  "Nahániri! Ñanderu."
  "Mama."
  "Nahániri."
  "Hummingbird was there in the beginning, che, Antonio."
  "No. You're telling tales. You must listen to the word of God."
  "You are tales, che. God eats food."
  "No. God needs nothing."
  "Mba'érepa?"
  "Because all things are in Him, Michĩ. Like the tree in the
seed and the jungle in the tree."

"Nahániri. A tree is not jungle."

"The Lord made the world, Mitākuña."

"Mba'érepa?"

"Well, I don't know. Because he wished to."

"Mba'érepa?"

"He was lonely, che?"

"I don't know. Perhaps he was."

"So he does need."

"Perhaps, Mitākuña."

"Sapucai, che! The hummingbird gives her food."

Mitākuña sets a pot of water on the fire. She adds clusters of small red fruits from a bush: añá-kti, she calls them. The water darkens into blood. It simmers. All three of them sing. *Oh, before before, the first first hummingbird, little birdie rehegua, the fruits of paradise, before before, to our auntie the first auntie, pretty little birdie, fly, fly, hummingbird.* Mitākuña removes the pot from the flames. The water is intensely red. She dips her fingers into it. Orders Antonio to undress again. He ends up in his underclothes, and again they paint him. Antonio is a map once more. Once more carved with rivers, lakes, mountains, and chasms, all red this time. It crosses his mind that what they're doing with him is some kind of ceremony. He likes it, he lets it happen. Who knows if these girls could deliver him into the world anew. How blindly he's been making his way, *before before, the first first birdie.* They leave him be for a while.

The sun has set, dear aunt. The animals shriek in the twilight. The girls draw their strange signs onto the earth. The monkeys linger, strangely motionless. And I yet owe you, I have not forgotten the list of my crimes. Let me tell you first that I survived a shipwreck and suffered the fevers of the tropics and was delivered from them by a black slave and buggerer, Cotita, in the shop that was my first site of American employ. And now for my first death, the death I dealt, the one I hastened in someone for whom, of course, my dear, it was already written, as it is written for everyone and everything. It was like this; I found myself in Saña, in the viceroyalty of Upper Peru, and I had gone, cured of my fevers and established as a shopkeeper, to the comedy, for a man must rest and make merry, as I know you will concede. My life was placid and serene, my dear. I brought books here and there, sold and accounted, granted credit to those patrons specified by my master and accounted for them in turn, purchased goods and accounted for them also. And that day, which was a feast day, I went to the comedy. I was in my seat when one Reyes sat right in front of me, close by, and sporting a hat with a brim so broad that he blocked my view. I addressed him in a most courteous tone, and he replied in the worst; "Cuckold," he said, and threatened to slash my face. O aunt, this was the man who provoked me. Either my manhood provoked me, or my honor, or both, who knows, perhaps it was written that I would leave that place, and my friends would pacify me; that I would return on Monday to the shop as I did on every Monday, and see Reyes walk past the threshold, then past it again; that I would seize a knife, go to the barber, ask him to grind and notch it to a jagged edge, gird my sword, the first I ever wore, and come upon Reyes with another man outside the church, and shout to him:

"Ah, Lord Reyes!"

"What do you want?"

"This is the face you would slash."

I sliced him on the slant, a cut that required ten stitches. His friend unsheathed his sword and set upon me, we grappled together, I stabbed my blade clean through his side, and there he fell. Just like that, my dear; brief and swift as I am telling it to you now, perhaps briefer and swifter still. I entered the church, but the magistrate pursued me and dragged me out, and that was my first night of

American imprisonment, stocked and shackled. The night was long, my beloved, but not my sentence, for my master traveled all the way back from Trujillo and undertook a thousand maneuvers to get me out; then I was restored to the church and confined there for three months, when the quarrel was resolved. The man I had felled would lose a great deal of blood, yet would not perish.

"Hey, che, be still."

"I am still."

They draw him now. Antonio's torso fills with geometric patterns. Mitākuña murmurs in her language. He doesn't know, Antonio, what this game is about. He lets them play it. They finish, or tire, and leave. Singing, so he can hear them: they sing all day long, and louder when they stray. The horses aren't coming back. Hopefully they've found their plains for grazing. These jungles are no place for steeds.

My master intended to marry me off, my aunt, to his own sweetheart, a cousin to Reyes himself, so as to spare me further troubles, though I did not wish it; stubbornly he advocated for the maid's fine qualities and the convenience of the union, and he sent me off to visit her at home, where she insisted on sleeping in my chambers and I refused, locking myself inside them; I had no choice but to lay hands on her so I could flee, and I told my master that by no means would I proceed with this marriage, and he accepted my will and transferred me to another shop. I set out for Trujillo, to begin anew, or so I thought, a righteous life following this sinful episode. After two months of laboring in the shop of my master, as diligently as I had worked in Saña, a slave alerted me to several men in the doorway who appeared to be carrying bucklers, I got word to a friend, the friend came to my aid, we emerged from the shop, and they attacked us at once. Fate had my sword pierce one man straight through, slaying him this time. My friend dashed to the church, where I was apprehended; and yet, when the magistrate inquired who I was and where I came from, and when I replied that I was Biscayne, he suggested to me in my native tongue that I should run when we passed the house of God. I did, my dear aunt, and there I remained until the arrival of my master, who followed my trial and secured my release once more. He paid my wages, fit me with two sets of clothes, and sent me off to Lima. And from then onward, and until this very moment, my life was like a boulder tumbling down a precipitous slope. Lurching and swift, brutish, blind, and deaf-mute have I lived, knowing almost nothing of this world, dear aunt, but what a hunted animal can know; but what is known by a deer who has served as breakfast for a jaguar and her cubs, and lunch for a vulture. Yet I have not been a deer. I have been a fearsome beast, aunt. And I killed for my honor or for my life, or because I was a soldier or because I was already falling as a landslide falls, killing and killing on its downward course, and who could ever stop such a thing? A song, dear aunt, two ashen girls, a dream uttered aloud, a promise poorly made. An orange, beloved.

26

They arrive distraught. Pale. Vacant-eyed, or seeing something only they can see, likely hell itself. It took the platoons many days and many dead before they found even so much as a nugget. The jungle Indians had no gold. But the two surviving soldiers—of the total hundred sent—found three who did, and brought them back. Second Lieutenant Gato, seated in the captain's office, orders them to be tended to, bathed, and fed. Then he gets right down to it. He confronts the Indians, asking where they got their gold. As they don't speak Castilian and can't reply, Gato calls in two slaves as his interpreters. As they claim not to know, he has them dragged out of his office, the captain's office, into the interrogation room. Straight onto the rack. His men shackle their ankles and their wrists to the wheels that turn in opposite directions. He attends in person. And sits before them. As they persist in their ignorance, he gives them a turn. As they persist in persisting, now weeping and begging for mercy, he gives them another turn. And another. And another. One swears the gold came down like rain in his village. Gato has this one quartered turn by turn. Everyone knows that it can't rain gold. Beholding his fellow's fate, the other says he got it from an Inca in the mountains. Gato releases him. He orders his body tethered to a stick to keep him upright. They chain him to the saddle of a horse and a platoon follows him into the hills. The last one swears he found the gold under the roots of certain trees that grow on the riverbanks and are particularly beautiful to behold. They smell of paradise. Their very flowers seem to be made of gold. Small and clustered, as intensely yellow as the sun. He'd even show them where they are. Gato has a hunch that this one is telling the truth. Everyone knows that gold is often found somewhere between earth and water. He sends the man to rest and to be treated by the tooth puller. There will be time to visit those trees and their golden blossoms. He returns to the captain's chambers, to administer his teas, his spoonfuls of mush. Simpering prick. Fucking buggerer. It's been almost two weeks and Ignacio's still laid up. But Gato does like reading to him from this most entertaining book.

I say that he was tied to the oak, naked from the waist up, and a peasant, who I learned later was his master, was beating him with the reins of his mare; as soon as I saw this I asked the reason for so savage a thrashing; the villain replied that he was beating him because he was his servant, and that certain of his careless acts were more a question of thievery than simplemindedness, to which this child said: "Señor, he's only beating me because I asked for my wages." The master answered with all kinds of arguments and excuses, which I heard but did not believe. In short, I obliged the peasant to untie him and made him swear that he would take him back with him and pay him one real after another, even more than he owed ...

"Everything that your grace has said is very true," responded the boy, "but the matter ended in a way that was very different from what your grace imagines."

"What do you mean, different?' replied Don Quixote. "Do you mean the peasant did not pay you?"

"He not only didn't pay me," responded the boy, "but as soon as your grace crossed the wood and we were alone, he tied me to the same oak tree again and gave me so many more lashes that I was flayed like St. Bartholomew, and with each lash he mocked you and made a joke about how he had fooled your grace, and if I hadn't been

feeling so much pain, I'd have laughed at what he said. But the fact is he raised so many welts that until now I've been in a hospital because of the harm that wicked peasant did to me. Your grace is to blame for everything, because if you had continued on your way and not come when nobody was calling you or mixed into other people's business, my master would have been satisfied with giving me one or two dozen lashes, and then he would have let me go and paid me what he owed me.

"As you can see, good Gato, it is quite impossible to help anyone. To help him, you must bring him to live with you. You live with me, little Gato. Therefore I must help you."

"Let's hope not like Don Quixote, boss."

Guffawing, the two men usher the night to its end. Tomorrow will come. And so will the time to tell the captain about the gold. Soon. Once he's found a little. He can already picture himself in a captain's garb: a bona fide Spaniard by rights, and by dint of gold.

27

Antonio no longer wears his garments. He's painted from head to toe with pink rivers and black lightning and red stripes. They cover almost all of him. Even his scars are nearly concealed. He wears only his underclothes now, a scrap of cloth once white, now brown with dirt. Is he no longer a gentleman? He hums. Bathes in the river. Eats the food of the Indians whose songs, he just now notices, are changing. The women and children sing less and less. And the men sing more. They sound like war, these songs. Should he worry? The girls must be protected. He decides to make a tree house in a neighboring tree, not the same yvyrá pytá that has granted them shade and shelter on sweltering afternoons, but another of its kind some five hundred paces off; a fine place, screened by flowers and plants with large leaves and roots, good for hiding little girls. He shares his plans with Mitākuña. She finds them reasonable. They gather boughs and broad leaves and bowls. Antonio, for his part, hones his dagger and his sword. He cleans his harquebus and musket. He laments that Orchid and Milk have not returned. Although he likes to imagine them roaming free. Galloping. They also begin to gather stones. Michī collects tiger ants in a coconut. It's a good idea. Except they escape, climb up her arms and bite her flesh. She cries. Antonio soothes her. She unknots herself from his embrace. Runs to a thicket. Plucks a leaf. Rubs it on her welts. Antonio watches them vanish. He thinks it can't be possible. If it weren't for his haste, he'd stop to investigate this and Michī's skin. But he doesn't stop. Maybe he'd be better off climbing the rocks, the smooth black boulders that shore up the cascades. Slipping behind them to where the Jesuits live. It would be easier to return to Spain from there, he thinks. He could bring the girls. Make princesses of these two lovely little beasts. He needs to think about it. It doesn't seem urgent. He forgets. *The first lightning thunder before before cools the mouth of mama, before before.* Time to write.

Oranges also fall. And roll away, my dear, as I have done. All the way to Lima, as it happened. I wish I could describe it, vaguely I recall its grandeur, a reminder of what Spain had been. Yet a strange Spain, teeming with gold that hinted at signs of another world, the world of the Indians running to and fro, heads ever bowed, and of their blood, with the gold gleaming darkly as it always does in the dim convents, the churches, the university, the archbishopric. Yet I found myself unable to truly see them, the Indians, through the splendor heralded by gold, and the hunger it tends to stir, urgent yet ethereal, the likes of which do not govern me. Gold never governed me. The open road governed me, a frenzy for fleeing, for the chase. Sometimes I believe I have lived the life of a hare in a field full of dogs. Yet then I remember how many dogs I butchered and left strewn along the road. In Lima, none. I didn't stay for long, although I had established myself in a new shop with a new master and worked there to our mutual satisfaction. My master had a wife and his wife two maiden sisters who took a fancy to me, dear aunt. Yes, I shall admit what you must have supposed by now: maids fancied me as they once fancied your brother, my father. And as they may have fancied you too, comely as you were, and must still be, as beautiful and regent, as splendid and as fierce a prioress as you have always been. Do you have fancies, dear aunt, of your own accord? I do. Not on that occasion, for I found myself with my head resting in the lap of one such maid, the one partial to combing my hair, and there I was, between her legs, when my master passed by.

*O aunt, if only I had not neglected to shut the windows! Or indeed
if only I had been patient enough to wait two days for my master's
fury to subside instead of hastening off to the militia, to join the
six companies setting forth for Chile. After three days, my master
wished for my return. Yet I let myself be swept along, my dear, by
my desires, which have always governed me above all other things,
and which I may have lost or may have not, I am not yet certain; I
wanted to roam and see the world. And I did roam, I have roamed.
But I saw little. Now I see, my dear; the girls draw upon my body.
They tell me how the world was made, they believe a goddess made
it, one fed by a hummingbird. The eldest says the creator is a mother.
The littlest objects, says it was a father. But neither disputes the
hummingbird. My body is completely painted, whether for war or
for a baptism I cannot say, perhaps the girls shall turn me into one
of them. I suspect they are witch children. We must not return to
Spain, it pains me to tell you. They would be burned at the stake.*

"Hey, che, it is a good óga."

"If you see anyone else who looks like me, go hide over there."

"Héē, che. They will not know you."

"Perhaps that is for the best, Mitākuña."

"Mba'érepa?"

"Because he took you from the cage, che, Michī."

"Mba'érepa?"

"He promised the Lady, the mama of God."

"Mba'érepa?"

"I do not know. Hey, che, why?"

"Think nothing of that. They will not find us."

28

Now it's time. The captain is upright in his chambers. Gato brings him his garments. Pours his tea. Draws the comb until his bald spot is neatly covered. He reminds Gato of Don Quixote, again. Ignacio is melancholy in spite of his laughter. He's displeased by the theater of power; he's weary. But if he doesn't rise and order death, if he doesn't remain vertical during the entire execution, then how will he uphold his authority? God knows that he would rather bathe in the river. Spend the day floating like a water hyacinth, snacking on grapes as his new secretary reads to him from that terribly funny book. Gato informs him of the men's work. How almost all have undertaken interminable labors to rectify their faults. How they have captured gold-bearing Indians. How they have forced the Indians to speak. How one has consequently disclosed that under certain golden-blossomed trees on the banks of a certain river, there are nuggets to be found. How only two of the hundred soldiers have returned. How they're mute and white as ghosts. How terror has gulped them down, held them in its entrails. How in this land, the Indians sing and are notable marksmen. Ignacio commands him to be silent. But then he asks what he meant by "almost all." Gato explains that there's a group of rebels among the men. Their leader is called Domínguez, and they demand to return to Spain. They'd prefer the wretchedest prison over this jungle. They refuse to go looking for more gold, all they seem to find is death. Gato lies. Domínguez and the rest have humiliated him more than once. Fucking Indian, they called him, and buggerer too. The captain is indifferent. Some must be executed: these men or others, it doesn't matter. He orders Gato to get the troops in formation in the square. And to have the Indians heat the drums. In the usual spot. By the gallows. He imagines the trembling of the soldiers. He exhales abundantly and stops keeping track of his breath. He's reflecting on how relieved the Indians must be. For one thing, there's no music at their executions. For another, what soldier hasn't committed an offense against them, a beating, an act of torture? The Indian slaves must dream up legions of drums to beat and beat for each and every such brute. They keep making more drums every night, painting them with pindó palms. Yarará snakes. The entire jungle. Depicting their monsters on the hides. Demons fashioned from animal parts with the bodies of men. To invoke them, spur them to blows, launch them straight into the white death that arrived on ships. They paint with invisible ink, the heathen schemers. Lines of lava that ignite when they play the gallows music.

The captain catches the scent of cooling skins like an order from above. He strides purposefully into the day. Crossing the threshold of his chambers, the sun distresses his vision. Time to fulfill his duty. What he wouldn't give to spend the whole day twiddling his thumbs. He cedes nothing. He is a nobleman and a soldier. First and foremost, he must ensure respect for authority, and respect it himself on nearly all occasions. Even understanding, as he understands, his men's repulsion for Indian rotgut. Their longing for Rioja. The itch for some festivity that would let them forget, if only for a little while, this fecund ground. These fevers. This treachery nesting in every branch, in every pair of eyes. Even in the spiders' eyes, which number more than a pair. He marches, the captain, toward his captainly endeavors in the center of the square. In formation, his soldiers blanch. They have had time enough to aggrandize, collectively, the misdeeds of the ephemeral secretary. The fugitive. They are tormented by a desperate wish to remain uneaten by vultures. Our Father who art in Heaven. Let it not be me tonight. Betrayal lurks among the brothers-at-arms. Among those who fought side by side. The captain is convalescing. His eyes sink into the violet hollows around them. His strength will leave him soon, God willing. He speaks:

"Domínguez, you swine. And you, who should have known not to swill a year's worth of wine on a night of mourning, as if it were a pagan feast. And you as well."

There could be more. He could send half the regiment to the gallows, the entire regiment, and it would be called justice. But to be left alone amid these jungles! The condemned have been fettered. They plead, in vain, for mercy. They remind their fellows that they saved their lives. Shared their final scraps of bread. Flasks in the desert. Overcoats in the snow. What shouts is the body. Their souls know their guilt. They found no crack in the conviction that they would do as the others are doing now, had they suffered the same fate.

"Confession!" Gato barks in his harsh New World accent. His chiseled cheekbones and eyes of surprising green. Eyes neither Spanish nor Indian. Eyes that seem to issue a Cain-like warning. It's the first time Ignacio has seen them in daylight. Gato brings him a chair, water, and succulent fruits. Offers him a new tea.

"Allow me, captain."

And he takes the first sip. And then another. And then another still. The captain livens up and drinks the rest. Begins to feel better. The new energy of the new tea traveling into his bloodstream grants him the vigor to command the imprisonment of two more men. The most bilious of the lot. A cripple and a one-eyed sort he never liked. He feels the urge to hang one of the little priests; how clever of Antonio to have scheduled them in shifts. But he restrains himself. One must choose one's battles. More shrieks and insults. He has some fun. Restoring order can be dull when ceremonious. But ceremony has its charms. He feels the sickly body of his troops healing along with his own. More pleas and curses. In vain, he thinks, growing vainer. They crash harmlessly into the parapets of his duty. His whole army sustained by him alone. What other reason for his men's obedience? What prevents the dolts from rebelling right then and there, far from the world? He does. Spain. What a pleasing tea. What a boon, this American Gato. The drums sound so furiously that the birds all but darken the sun as they scatter in the sky. Seated, the captain general beholds the executions. Once again, they make him retch.

"Mercy's a Christian virtue, boss, am I right? And what's more Christian than obedience. The Lord rewards our service to the King, our king. The king of Christendom. He'll give you bread and teeth and shiny medals for you to pin on your chest after dinner. Come on, boss, have some more tea. Just wait and see, it'll heal the pain of duty done."

A bit unctuous, this American, pretending to mistake a hangover for divine mercy. Yet a good physician and a good reader, as he has amply proven. The captain commands him to have a platoon escort the Indian who claims there's gold under the roots of the trees. The second tea quells his disgust at the scene. Now, at last, he can return to his chambers, then retreat to the river later on. Gato and the most loyal soldiers can bathe in his company. Then they can play cards and sing. He calls for a tablecloth, food, and wine. There's still a little left over.

29

The girls want to know. They wake. They peel apart the bud they form together when they sleep. They stand and ask. About everything.

"Hey, che, why do they burn?"

"Why do they burn what?"

"People."

"Mba'érepa?"

"Well, because they have sinned before God."

"Does God like it, che?"

"The fire purifies, Mitākuña. And it pleases God."

"Do they eat them?"

"No! Only brutes eat people."

"What are roots?"

"Mba'érepa?"

"You two, and your kind."

"We are brutes in the roots?"

"Yes."

The Indians' songs have grown fiercer and fiercer. They make his war wounds sting all over his body. He also feels the itch to write. Everything is ready. He's gotten dressed again, although he hasn't washed off the paint, not even from his face. The girls know they'll have to climb the tree. And flee through the canopy to their kin. Because their families are nearby, Mitākuña has told him, so they're safe. But the voices. The warlike singing. They're safe, the girl insists, and Antonio believes her for now. Although the magpie who visits them each day is screaming. Magpies speak. They warn of danger. Danger is near. He needs to finish what he's promised. Will his letter ever reach his aunt? Will he convey it himself, with his girls dressed like princes and he as an Indian king? He'd better write.

I would see nothing. Not even what I most dearly yearned to see that night, the darkest of my soul, when I couldn't see, when I saw nothing, aunt. I shall be swift in my telling, swift as the times that shot through me. And not only the times. Onward, onward, no more circles, I will tell you; swiftly I found myself in the kingdom of Chile. Such was my fate that roll was called by Miguel de Erauso, my own elder brother, whom I never knew, as he left when I was but two years old, yet of whose existence I was aware. He took roster, asked names and origins, and when I said I was Biscayne, he embraced me and greeted me in that tongue, for he had not encountered a sole compatriot since he departed Spain. I became a soldier under his command, dining for three years at his table, reveling in a brotherhood as previously unknown to me as it would be secret; for only I would know it. I had to reforge myself in his affection, a love I believed withheld from me since my flight from your side, an impossible love, dear aunt, the love of family, the love of mutual protection, the love of the place to which one returns. After all, where would I return to, and how? To your side? What would a man do, a soldier, in a convent? I had my brother. Yet on occasion I accompanied him to the house of a lady he kept there and who had taken a fancy to me, and I returned alone on other occasions, and once he saw me and awaited me outside the door and attacked me, and thus I was forced to defend myself. The governor heard tell of it and sent me into the inferno of Paicabí, where my hands ever clutched their weapons amid the fierce war waged upon us by the Araucanos. It is curious, dear aunt; war staves off all proscriptions, even those of women. I never bled again thereafter. Five thousand strong on the Valdivia plains, we weathered great trials, yet in the end we vanquished our enemies and inflicted grave destruction upon them over the course of four assaults. Until the fifth, when we were thrashed; they killed many among us, including captains and even my lieutenant, my dear, and seized our flags. Even wounded in one leg, I followed them, slayed the cacique who bore that flag aloft, and trampled others under the hooves of my horse, endlessly maiming, crushing, and killing. I myself was grievously wounded; pierced by three arrows and a spear cleaved into my left shoulder, which caused me considerable pain. Some returned for me, including my brother, which was a great solace. Oh, Miguel. My convalescence lasted nine months and he spent each and every day beside me. When this spell was over, my brother hoisted the flag I had recovered and made me a lieutenant, dear aunt. Five years I served as such.

"Hey, che, what is soul?"

"Mba'érepa?"

"Ah. Well, it is the spirit of a person, Mitākuña. Because it is, Michī."

"What is spirit?"

"Like Ka-ija-reta, which is there but cannot be seen, the incorruptible part that does not die. Now leave me be. Go sing."

"Are you root, che?"

"I don't know, Mitākuña. Go for a walk. Sing."

"And your oranges, che? Why do you not look for them?"

"Look for them yourselves. Singing."

"Mba'érepa?"

"You know why, Michī."

I found myself in the battle of Purén, where my captain was slain, and passed six months at the head of my company, engaging Indians in several encounters and enduring wounds from their arrows. In one such fray, I stumbled upon a christened Indian captain and

did battle with him, and I toppled him from his horse, and he sur-
rendered. As he had killed many of ours, and as I was captive to
fury and grief, I had him hanged from a tree. The governor had
wanted the man to be brought back alive, and resented me for his
execution, and so he refused to grant me command of the company,
and gave it instead to another captain, promising that he would
authorize my return to Concepción as soon as the opportunity arose.
Like a rock, as blind and deaf and dumb, I fell and fell, my dearest,
convinced of my forward progress, though without so much as a
horizon before me. How can one advance without direction? What
could advancement mean if not from here to there?

But oh, dear aunt, O Fortune! How she turns chance encounters
into destiny. Finding myself idle in Concepción one day, I crossed the
path of another lieutenant in a nearby gambling house. We began to
play, and the game unfurled, the liquor flowed, and in a disagree-
ment that ensued, with many others present, he claimed I lied like
a cuckold. Instantly my sword pierced his chest. Many assailed me,
so many that I couldn't move. The local judge questioned me, and I
replied that I would only make my statement before the governor,
and they struck me, and then my brother appeared and urged me in
Biscayne to run for my very life. The judge seized me by the neck;
dagger in hand, I told him to release me, and shook him off and dealt
him a blow, slashing his cheeks, and then he grabbed me again, and
I slashed him again, and broke loose. I drew my sword, many others
lit upon me, I withdrew to the doorway, dodging obstacles here and
there, and departed for the San Francisco convent, which was close
by, where I ascertained that both judge and lieutenant were dead.
The governor came forth and shuttered the church for six months,
with me inside. His proclamation pledged a reward for my capture
and warned no port to grant me embarkation; however, over time,
which heals all wounds, his severity softened and he called off the
guards he had posted. My state of alarm too eased and I began to

feel more settled, receive more visitors. I endeavored to reform, again, and begin anew, abstain from cards and players, converse with the priest, stroll in the forest, read, and fish. Everything, my dear, to stave off my old ways.

Yet it was then that my lieutenant friend appeared and told me that he had exchanged words with another, and challenged him to a duel that very night, at eleven o'clock, for which each must bring a second. I felt wary and uncertain, to which he said: If you are not with me, then so be it; I shall go alone, for I trust no other man. And I thought, What is it that gives me pause? And, hapless, I accepted.

After prayers, I departed the convent for my friend's house. We dined and talked, of what, you may wish to know, of what do two men talk as they are dining mere minutes before they kill or die, and I, dear aunt, I could not tell you; I don't recall. Trifles, I believe. Regardless, when the clock struck ten, we set out for the spot.

"It never dies, che, the spirit soul?"

"No, Mitākuña."

"Mba'érepa?

"Because it does not, Michī. The body dies, not the soul."

"It goes with God, with the root angels?"

"Mba'érepa?"

"Well, it does if it confesses, yes. Angels are not brutes."

"Mba'érepa?"

"Because they are not, Michī. Because a brute is bad and foolish."

"Nahániri!"

"Why foolish?"

"Because he does not know Lord God our Father, nor horses, nor the worth of gold, nor weapons, nor the king, Mitākuña."

"Why bad?"

"Well, for the same reasons."

"Nahániri!"
"Nahániri!"
"Let me write a little longer."

So dark was the night that we could not see our hands. Why tell you, aunt, of every lunge. My friend went down, and his enemy as well, and the pair of us left standing then parried on, until my sword entered him, I later learned, beneath the left breast. Struck from the ground.

"Ah, traitor, it seems you have slain me."

So did the fallen man cry out and beg for confession. Yearning not to recognize the voice I recognized, I asked his name. Miguel de Erauso, he said. Shattered by a bolt of lightning, not yet accepting what I knew to be true, I fled. How is it that pain can strike one down not in the instant of the wound, beloved aunt, but later? I made it to the San Francisco convent, which was but a short distance away, sent for two priests, and I fell swifter and swifter, breaking and breaking more and more, if there could exist a steeper fall, a sharper splintering. I was already fallen. How could I have kept roaming as I did? Battered as I was. Deserving every blow.

30

"Alive. Bring me the traitor alive."

"Going to wring his neck yourself, huh, captain?"

"Be still, imbecile, and follow your orders in silence."

The new secretary neither bristles nor frets: he knows where he's going. And how high his ladder looms. He climbs. He thinks of nothing but the towering heights that will spare him from being spat upon. Even if he's forced to scale them drenched in phlegm. Skidding on the mucus emitted by any one of these louts. Take this moron, the captain. Lord Combover the Spare—that's what they must have called him where he's from. He sends out another platoon, ten men on ten horses, the sharpest-looking of the lot. He must be close by, his fugitive predecessor. Fucking madman. Why bother stealing Indians on this red earth, aswarm as it is with them? The crest, the sword, the bag, two little Indian girls, two horses. A irremediable blockhead. A total idiot. He must be around here somewhere. Who knows, maybe he's founding a new kingdom. The crest, the sword, the Indians. He'll need more Spaniards and a priest. Maybe others are waiting for him. Hiding out there in the jungle. And how does he intend to found a new kingdom with the same crest, the same sword, the same Indians, the same Spaniards? Sooner or later, he'll get to interrogate the rogue ex-scribe. Now it's time to head into the brush, find more herbs for Lord Cowlick, who'll be stirring soon. He's stuck here on the bottom rungs. Why does he want the traitor alive?

Antonio is not, it's true, very far away. Even less far is the platoon: night is falling, the insects are biting, the torches blaze in thousands of eyes, gleaming as if the torchlight lived inside them. Like will-o'-the-wisps.

"Why are they singing? What do they sing of?"

"Of war, what else, you half-wit. They are nowhere near, pay more mind to where you tread. There will be snakes afoot."

"I have already told you, they frighten the horses."

"And I've told you that I slit one open and found an entire horse inside. Barely digested. Looked like an unborn babe."

"That was no serpent from here."

"It was, man, just as we arrived. Good God, I've told you a thousand times already."

"They will go lame on us. One cannot gallop in the jungle."

"Let's tie them. And continue on foot."

"We may as well slice them to ribbons and toss them to the beasts, you fool. It would be like tying up lambs in wolf country."

"What trash, the singing secretary."

"Well indeed he …"

He doesn't finish. The soldier keels instantly to the ground carpeted in ferns. A small red flower blooms from his throat. A dart. The others throw themselves down beside him, under the horses. Three more soldiers burgeon with red blossoms. A legion of blue worms wriggle into the flowers.

"Our Father who art …"

"This is no time for prayers. Hand me the harquebus."

"Go get it yourself, I won't feed myself to the worms."

"Give it here, imbecile, or I shall have you hanged for treason, as I am your lieutenant."

"And my kid brother."

"Give it here."

With his brother's dagger at his throat, the eldest inches out. Groping for the saddle, his white hand flowers too with death.

The harquebus drops to the ground and fires. The bullet strikes the younger brother in the face. The dead shudder and deflate, bones creaking. Five are left. They barely dare to breathe. The vulture plunges, spiraling toward its prey as vultures do before tearing their supper to shreds. But it doesn't get there. It perceives the five men's panicked breathing. Returns to the sky, coasts serenely. It never lacks for food. It never lacks for anything. The world unfurls at its talons, crazed with beauty. And the pale men fill it with food. Satisfied, it watches the warhorses drift slowly away. An Indian leads them. The five soldiers will have to walk. But they treasure the distinction: they're breathing, not like their flowered fellows mutating into stew dregs spilled onto the ground. They turn. Start marching toward the barracks in the greatest silence they've ever kept. All in vain. They don't know where the darts are coming from. One blossoms, then another, then the other three. Their wide eyes gaze into the vultures' heaven.

31

Antonio suggests new songs. Songs of thanks, he says. Mitākuña and Michī wish to hear them.

Good Indians who keep us nicely fed
on muburucuyá, manioc, and honey
Kind Indians who keep us safe from harm
Let's travel to the sea, let's go to the sea together

The girls don't like the song. They suggest spells against the enemy instead.

"And who is the enemy?"

"Ones like you, che."

"And what of me?"

"You?"

"Not I, certainly."

"Mba'érepa?"

"Because I am not the enemy, Michī. How do those spells work, then?"

The girls begin to sketch geometric patterns on their skin. Pink ink from the yvyrá pytá tree. Antonio contributes his own, a cross, which is also geometric, he notes, and a fish.

"These are the spells I learned as a boy."

The spells are necessary. He's no longer astonished by the golden fireflies that flutter around the girls whenever he opens his eyes after keeping them shut for a moment. Nor by Michī doing whatever she's doing. Standing. Taking two steps. And with the third, following the same rhythm, she appears in the fronds of a palm. Or on the tallest rock on the bank of the stream. Now, for example, she's calling out to him. She's rolling around in a patch of luminous ferns. This doesn't astonish him, either. The green light cast by the ferns in this jungle.

Such blows were surely fierce, my dear aunt. Yet so dark was the dark night of my own soul that I could not feel them, I felt nothing, not even the desire to save my own life. Yet I did save it every time. Until I found myself here, in this jungle made of green light, of tree air, of glistening water. I would flee Concepción eight months after I heard the "Ah, traitor" of my elder brother, slain by my own hand, seeing only the night in which I could not even see the hand that slayed him. Yet I would walk on. To Valdivia and up above, into the mountains, resolved to anything but my own capture. I walked with two other men who shared my resolve; I didn't know, my aunt, on account of what crimes, though they could hardly be worse than my own, as I expect you will agree. We climbed and climbed and there were no more animals or grass, just meager roots to keep us living. I would have rather fled through a jungle, yet one flees down whichever path is clearest, and the only path that lay before me was over mountains. We killed one of our horses, yet the poor creature was only skin and bones, its meat served us little, yet it was all we had for sustenance. We did the same with the others. Their look of sorrowful surprise, resigned and dear and gentle, when met with the knife. On the fifth day, we glimpsed two men and were cheered. Until we reached them and found them dead, frozen stiff, with a grimace on their faces like a smile. We were frightened. Yet not from fear alone did the first of us perish, but from cold and hunger. And on the next day the other also perished and I was still walking. With what strength, beloved aunt, with what determination? How could I resist this frigid death? The sweetness of a return to the cradle, of being swaddled by your aunt, by your mother, by your sister: this I saw in the smiles of my companions.

"Hey, che, what is confession?"

"When you commit a sin and tell it to the priest and he forgives you. And that is that."

"Mba'érepa?"

"Because the priest is the representative of God and may forgive your sins. Weren't you in the ferns, little one?"

"She came back, che. What is shin?"

"A sin is when you kill or lie or steal."

"Mba'érepa?"

"Because it is."

"It is bad to lie and steal and kill, Michī, che."

"Mba'érepa?"

"I don't know."

I went on, bearing my harquebus, my remaining scrap of horse meat, eight pesos I found in the pockets of my final dead companion, and the certainty of sharing his fate. I huddled against a tree, a tree, dear aunt, not realizing I was descending, had made my way almost entirely down below, and I wept. I wept as I hadn't wept since I was expelled from my father's house; as a little boy I wept, as a little girl. As a man. As I never wept again. I prayed a rosary, invoked the Holy Virgin and her husband, the glorious Saint Joseph. I rested between bouts of weeping and praying and praying and weeping. Then I walked on, walked until I had left the kingdom of Chile and entered Tucumán. I saw two living men, and they saw me, and I saw they were Christians, and I let myself fall. Onto the grass. Grass. Onto living ground I fainted, into the caressing breath of the earth, into its green fragrance. The men led me to their mistress, a half-breed lady, Indian and Spanish, well established and good-hearted, and to my great fortune she tended to me until I was well. She wanted me as a husband for her daughter, as there were so few Spaniards in that place, yet I did not share her wish; I have always been partial to beautiful women, and I was slow to understand the new beauty of America. I couldn't see it, my aunt. And marriage was never my wish. How would I roam if I were to marry? And how could I be spared the pyre? I fled Tucumán. Well dressed, and with horses of my own, all gifts from my benefactor. I ran. And that is what I am doing now, as I write these words; I go on, aunt, I gallop, I gallop, I must not stop until I have told you everything. Now to Potosí, which is far from Tucumán; three months of travel and two dead men, this is what it cost me to reach it. There I worked as a butler, but my master became embroiled in quarrels that led to garnishments and shackles. I had my own share of troubles, so I left his side. I found myself once more in the militia, enmeshed in battles between Indians and Christians. We conquered a village, beloved aunt, flush with the gold sought by Columbus, our admiral. The river rose and sank and revealed three fingers of gold. We filled our hats and pockets. And for what, my dear, if I would only gamble it away and lose it then and there? The Indians had fled; we had wreaked great havoc upon them. A demon of a boy, some twelve years old, had stayed behind, hidden in a tree. When our captain looked up, an arrow pierced his eye. We tore him into a thousand pieces, aunt, and he was little more than a child. No one blamed me for it. Yet later I returned to a Christian village and was charged with a crime I did not commit: slashing a lady's face. I have never slashed a woman and do not think I ever will. I endured the rack, and their questions, aunt, the turning and turning, and was condemned to ten years behind bars, but in the end the truth was revealed and I managed to flee. It has been most taxing, my dearest, to write this out. I believe I am able to do so because of the girls, because of the little dog who seeks shelter in me, because of the monkeys who bring fruits to me, because of the songs. Yet, as you know, the songs of the Indians sound like war. The entire jungle pulses. I don't know what is coming. The girls have begun to mutter spells.

32

Ignacio is much recovered now. He felt strong at the gallows, light at the river. He drank and he ate. He joked with his men. Then he grew weary and retired to his chambers. Ordered Gato to sleep beside him. On the floor, for now. So he said. Gato reviews the conversation. There's no doubting what he heard, for now. He isn't sure he wants the promotion implied by the captain's turn of phrase. Much less to await it sleeping on the ground like a dog. He wants Gato close, the captain said, right beside him, for his teas and recitations. Fucking fag, thinks Gato. He fears the Indians: ever since they almost killed him, and as their belligerent singing grows closer and closer, he's been trembling. A hankering to be skewered, is what the captain general has. Or to do the skewering. He'll assent, of course, if he must. But he'll charge a pretty penny, he's already running the tab. It's the eyes, the hands, the captain's voice. All that fairy wants is to hightail it home. His transfer order has arrived. It revived his zeal.

"Gato, little Gato, just a little more gold: a few more chests of it and off I go."

The companies that embarked in search of gold, with the two Indians nearly quartered after their confessions on the rack, fail to advance even in their scattered state. Darts rain down, as if the trees had Indians for leaves. Obtuse ones at that. Disguised as leaves. The soldiers shoot upward. Not only darts but also Indians rain down. And arrows. And rocks. The marksmen are crushed and the projectiles intensify. The animals have fled. Birds cawing like a thunderhead. The larger mammals sprint or leap from branch to branch. The rodents dig. The reptiles swim or slither. Only plants and men are left. Howls. Crunching bones. Jets of blood soaking fruits, then fungi. There are no more ferns. There's no red earth left in the jungle. There's nothing but an upholstery of broken bodies that keep breaking, even in death, because they keep receiving the continuous impact of the newly fallen. The sound is discreet. Like half-empty wineskins dropping onto half-empty wineskins. A deep plop or ploff. In the background. Like the stridencies of the cicadas that haven't gone, but are now barely audible. By contrast, the crunches and screams are deafening. The strewn limbs. The bodies impossible to reassemble into a single form. The souls departing. The blue worms chewing. The vultures blackening the sky in a throng of tragedy. The mushrooms manufacturing teeth to work more quickly. The animals sniffing danger and food from afar. Little by little, the battle quiets. There are three Spaniards left alive. Eyes open. Mouths closed. The Indians retreat. They leave the jungle's work to the jungle. To eat it all. Take it into itself.

33

Maybe they aren't war songs. Although they sound like it. Maybe they're only taking turns. Maybe the men are singing to the sun god. And the women and children to the moon god. But there were no celestial-body gods in what Mitākuña told him. Maybe they're singing all the songs they know. Maybe it's an Indian holiday, like the Nativity or Easter. In any case, the tree house is ready and he spends half the day discouraging the girls:

"No, it's not a good idea to decorate it with flowers and feathers on the outside. It's a very nice idea to do so on the inside. Inside you may adorn it however you wish."

He climbs up to survey the result. The house is the palace of the queen of the butterflies, or the hummingbirds. Or both. Everything is colorful. Nothing is still. The breeze stirs the feathers and petals that glimmer and darken and glimmer again. It's a good place to wait for help, Antonio decides, if his fellows should come. Well, his former fellows. Even if they never truly were. He's always been a foreigner among his own. He spent a lifetime concealed behind garments, behind a new name, a new tale. Fleeing the flames. Almost always. When he traveled back to the old world, he no longer hid his true name or his true story. Nor did he know any longer what his true story was. Telling and retelling the one he'd written so the king would recognize his right to a pension, and so he'd look like someone worthy of a pension, disoriented him. He returned to America. Went back to being, yet again, anyone. To flee again, though he no longer needed to. Now, in this abiding, in this jungle, with these girls, these animals, in this state of being with no story and no name, he feels comfortable. He could stay here.

I set forth again, dear aunt. For Charcas, stumbling, endlessly falling, turned into a stone; I could no longer even bear the "Ah, traitor" uttered by my brother, I could not even see the blackness of that night in the place where my hands must have been. The cards and drinks kept coming; I wager, what do you wager, I wager, what do you wager; daggers, friends intervening, the man awaiting me with his sword drawn on a shadowed corner, drawing my own, wounding each other, slaying him, fleeing once more. To Piscobamba. A friend received me, more cards, more drinks and more insults, companions interceding, the insulted man retreating, seemingly calmed. Yet three nights later, at around eleven, returning home, I spied a man standing on the corner; I swept back my cape to draw my sword and continued on my way. He charged me, called me a cuckold, and threw me to the ground; I pulled him down, my sword pierced him dead. I stayed beside him, in the pool of blood that spread like a tide, thinking what to do, he was a crag jutting over a red sea when I realized there was no one else about. I returned home, threw my shoes and breeches into the fire, and went to sleep when they had reduced to ash. The next morning, very early, the magistrate came, apprehended me, and escorted me to the jail. Within an hour, he returned with a scribe and took down my declaration. I denied it all. Witnesses came forth, faces I had never seen. They sent for a confessor, then another, then another still. Friar after friar, as if friars rained down from the sky to drown me, yet still I did not confess. What could I offer but silence, what save muteness in response, what else, my dear? No longer could I even pray, nor confess, nor commend myself to God and the Virgin, who had already done me too many favors. I was sentenced to death, bound for execution. They dressed me in a taffeta frock, and the friars said that if

I wished to go to hell, if I refused to confess, then I was free to do so, they would even procure me a horse for the trip. They removed me from the jail, lead me down unfamiliar alleys to thwart any impulse to escape. When I reached the gallows, the friars shrieked so stridently that I could not think, they shoved me up the four steps, I had to climb higher, they strung me with the noose, the thin cord used for hanging, yet the executioner failed to tie it properly. At last, I could speak. I told him, "You drunkard, either put it on or take it off." And finally, just as the drunkard was adjusting the rope, a messenger from the court of Ciudad del Plata came galloping in as if the archangel Gabriel himself were descending from heaven. I believe I heard trumpets, dear aunt. The miraculous mercy of God came to my aid. As it happened, they had apprehended the witnesses who had consigned me to my doom, and sent them to hang for some other crime altogether, and in their final confession, they revealed that they had been bribed to accuse me. I vowed to reform, to make myself worthy of the favor of God. They would free my neck from the noose, my beloved.

"Hey, che, if I make a shin, does the priest forgive me?"
   "Mba'érepa?"
   "Yes. Because God is good."
   "What if the priest is gone?"
   "Mba'érepa?"
   "Because he left, Michĩ, che."
   "Mba'érepa?"
   "Did he leave for the jungle?"
   "No, for hell."

And it would not be the last time I donned this fearful raiment.
   I must finish, I must hasten to the end. Of course, dear aunt, I left that place. I arrived in Cochabamba and encountered a woman

begging for help. Her slave explained to me that her husband had found her with another man, slain him, and locked her up to kill her later; he had gone for a drink with his fellows, as he was wont to discuss his affairs with them. Two passing friars urged me to assist her, and I agreed; they sat her down on the haunches of my mule, and we departed. Miraculously, we forded a roiling river, and there, though I know not how, for we had left a good while earlier, the husband was awaiting us with his musket. The bullets passed so close that they sliced through our hair, my dearest. We made it to the church, as did the husband. There he thrust the tip of his sword between my breasts. And I cleaved my dagger in his side. Many people came to separate us. Five months I was forced to spend in the care of the friars. You must wonder how none of the gentle souls who abetted me throughout my life has ever noted that I have the body of a woman. My dearest, I cannot say. Could it be another kindness done by God and the Virgin? Or perhaps no one sees what is not, even if it in some way is. In the end, the dispute was resolved; she to the convent, he to the monastery.

The lady secured for me, as compensation for services rendered, a post as sheriff of Piscobamba. There I apprehended a lieutenant who had robbed and treacherously slain two Indians, burying them in his garden. I sentenced the lieutenant and condemned the man to death. He appealed, his appeal was heard, and he was sent to the gallows regardless. Once the matter was closed, I continued to the city of La Paz. There I conversed with the servant of a friend, who challenged me and struck me in the face with his hat. Instantly I felled him. Again. I cannot say how many deaths lie strewn behind me.

"Into the fire, che?"

"Yes. Forever."

"Because of shins?"

"Mba'érepa?"

"I don't know, Michī."

They captured me, condemned me to death, took my confession, pardoned me, and granted me communion. Spitting out the host, I requested asylum from the church, which granted it. The governor had the church surrounded for an entire month, at which point he relaxed his vigilance. And I came to see Cuzco, was faulted for a death I had not caused, proved my innocence, and returned to Lima, city of strange, abundant gold. There I joined the battle against a Dutch privateer, who had sent his armada to thieve gold from the city. I survived a shipwreck, aunt, and celebrated the triumph of our forces. And I returned to Cuzco. I lodged in the house of a friend, cards and drink ensued, and the new Cid meddled with my winnings, a swarthy, hairy man of frightening mien. He palmed eight of my coins and departed and I let him. Yet he returned and dipped into my money once more. I whipped out my dagger and cleaved his hand into the table. His friends assailed me. Two Biscayne men passed by, glimpsed me in a truly dire state, and fought beside me; we were three against five, the worst came when the Cid pierced me through with his dagger. I fell in a sea of blood and all the others absconded. Yet I managed to raise myself, now covetous of death, and found the Cid in the threshold of the church. We set upon each other and I stabbed my dagger into his belly and he crumpled to the ground, begging to confess. I too fell. Fearing death, I confessed my entire life to a friar, who nursed me back to health. And now, dear aunt, and here, I dream by night. A tigress embraces the girls, bathes them in her golden halo, a holy tigress surely. When I wake, she is nowhere to be found. Yet fireflies flit about the little ones.

34

Two hundred men departed and only three returned. With neither gold nor Indians. Not even one of the two who'd been nearly torn apart on the rack. Ignacio and Gato confer. If the Indians are putting up such a fight, they must have something to defend. Something they don't want to lose. They can't think of anything but gold. They're soldiers. Not even honor crosses their mind. For honor, as they know, is weak. It capitulates when so much blood is at stake. Gold, then. They devise a new plan. If gold lies beneath the roots, then the trees must be uprooted. And the Indians. Nothing else to be done. They'll burn it all down. They'll use long ropes dipped in tar. They'll spray the jungle with chicha. They'll paint it with pitch. They'll riddle the trees. They'll start with smoke. They'll shoot fiery cannonballs. They'll set even the roots aflame. Especially the roots. Ah, fire, fire. Captain and lieutenant speak, gazing into each other's eyes. They toast, content. Clink for the return to town. Clink for Spanish America. Clink for friendship. The captain sitting up in bed, Gato on a stool beside him, both men contained in the triangle of light whose point they can't see, because they're looking at each other. Cat eyes, says Ignacio. General eyes, Gato responds. Come, my friend, come sit with me, the captain invites him. Helps him to stand. Hands clasped. They linger there together, asses perched on the mattress, feet planted on the floor. Valiant soldiers who don't know where to begin. Should the captain make the first move, being naturally in command? Gato hesitates: he wouldn't want to face a court-martial. Much less the ensuing pyre. Ignacio lays a hand on his thigh. My good friend, he says. Gato pounces like a jag-uar: turns him around, bites his neck, pulls down his breeches, his underthings.

"Slowly, Gato, slowly now. First you kneel."

And the officer sits up and looks down at him, the tip of his member dangling over Gato's head.

"Now lick."

Gato, gentle, sticks out his tongue, Gato opens his mouth, envelops the gland, lightly squeezes the balls. He feels how Ignacio grows feral, how he removes himself from his mouth, how he pushes him to the floor, how he takes Gato's cock and fills his own mouth with relish, how he tells him to stand, how the captain kneels, how his piggish ass protrudes, Gato grabs the captain by that ridiculous little mane of his, pries him off his cock, crushes his head against the ground, and skewers him now. He rises and falls and rises and falls inside the sweet captain until he loses himself and the other too is lost.

"Fire, Gato, fire."

"Fire, captain, so much fire."

"We shall burn it all down."

35

Antonio, who is writing to his aunt at this very moment, knows none of this. In the next moment, he stops. The girls call to him. Red requests his attention with her paw. Kuaru and Tekaka shimmy up his body and leap and shimmy up the vines and vault onto his head. They want to play. The girls have painted and painted his face. Hand in hand, they walk toward the palm trees, calling his name. They dance. He is supposed, he realizes, to dance in the middle. He does. He also realizes he's supposed to flaunt his paint. He stays in his undergarments. The girls jump all around him and speak in deep voices. Or try to. They're painted in red and black. Red stripes on their cheeks. Between their eyes. On their forearms. On their legs. Black geometric patterns across their foreheads. On their shoulders. They look very bright among the green branches, the trunks and vines and roots all different hues of brown, the exultant flowers, the eyes of the animals flashing fleetingly here and there.

"Hey, che, yvy marãe'ỹ."

"What is that?"

"Earth with nothing Evil in it."

"Go on."

"Dance first, che."

Antonio is the radial point of the dance, as if he were the sun, but not the sun that lances its formidable rays onto the parts of the jungle cleared of trees. A sun that receives rays, receives song. They sing to him, he thinks, what kind of song is this, a loving one, he supposes, because that's how they look at him, and because of their sweet voices. They sing to him a grateful love. Soon they must go. But Antonio doesn't know this, either. They dance and sing and dance until Antonio can dance no more and sits down in the middle of the circle. Little Red curls up in his lap. Licks his face. The girls hug him. The monkeys hug the girls. They always form a flower. A flower that sings. Until they smell the scent of food. Each girl runs toward her bowl. Mitākuña brings Antonio her own. At last they tire, lie down on the cape. Antonio returns to his task.

Death, dear aunt, lay in wait for me; I found myself captive in a labyrinth that seemed to have no exit. In every threshold, cards and flowing drink, shouting, daggers, swords, the rope around my neck. I galloped for leagues and leagues and in all directions I found everything the same, the whole vast New World a hall of mirrors where I discovered nothing but myself and the Reaper stalking me and the Reaper always setting the same trap. As in a comedy. I saw neither mountains nor jungles nor Indians nor tigers nor steppes nor stars; just cards and drink, curses and duels, blood and flight. Dead without dying is how I lived, my beloved, lost in an inferno of mirrors, as if I had already passed into the afterlife and the whole world were my sentence, my circle. Until I came to Guamanga. There I found an inn and stayed for several days. Disgrace, my aunt, or grace, must have wished me to push open the door of a gambling house; fate or the Reaper made such doors appear before me wherever I roamed, for one day the magistrate was there, and he looked upon me and didn't recognize me and asked me where I was from. From Biscay, I said. And where had I come from now? From Cuzco. He paused for a moment, looking upon me, and said, To prison with you.

"Earth with nothing Evil, che, is where the good ones go."
"Mba'érepa?"

"And what do they do there?"
"Eat oranges and dance. And do not die."
"I am most glad to hear it."

I drew my sword and made for the door, where I met with such resistance that I was repulsed. I pulled out a three-barrel pistol and went out and vanished, seeking refuge in the home of a friend. There I spent several days until things quieted down and it seemed, once again, of utmost urgency that I depart. In that moment, I possessed exactly what I had possessed at every other time; nothing, dear aunt. I left by night and at once happened upon two sheriffs who asked who goes there and I said the devil. Which I should not have said. Voices rose, shouting Seize him! The magistrate appeared, as he was lodging at the bishop's house, in the company of other ministers and many friars. In great distress, I fired my pistol and down one went. More joined the melee, and I found myself fighting alongside various Biscayne friends. The magistrate commanded them to slay me. Until the bishop emerged with four torchbearers and his secretary, who said to me, Lord lieutenant, give me your weapons. I replied, My lord, there are many adversaries here. He said, Give them to me, for you shall be safe in my care, and you have my word that I shall get you out, even if it should cost me my life. I said, Most Illustrious Lord, as soon as I am able I shall kiss your holy feet. His Eminence extended his arm to me, I surrendered my weapons, placed myself at his side, and entered his house. He saw that a small wound I had was tended, then sent me to bed with some supper, locking the door with a key he took away with him. I slept in peace. The next morning, around ten o'clock, His Illustriousness had me brought before him and asked me who I was, where I was from, who my father was, and the full course of my life and the incidents and forking paths that had conveyed me there. I began to tell him bit by bit, dear aunt, mixing truth with lies, although more truth than

lies, with certain omissions. I told him of the cards, the curses, the
duels, the prisons, the flights, the new cities, the cards again. America
itself a trifling circle to me. He dispensed fine and loving counsel.
And moved by his holiness, feeling myself in the presence of none
other than the Lord Himself, I revealed myself and said, My lord,
all that I have relayed to Your Illustrious Lordship is otherwise.
The truth is this; that I am a woman, daughter of So-and-So and
So-and-So; I was dispatched to the convent at a tender age, with
So-and-So my aunt; I was raised within its walls; I took the veil
and became a novice; on the verge of professing, I escaped; I fled
to such-and-such place, stripped, clothed myself, sheared my locks,
wandered about; I weighed anchor, reached port, roamed, slayed,
wounded, debauched, and roamed some more, until I found my way
into my present circumstances at the feet of Your Illustriousness.

The holy lord, as I related my entire life to him, or as much of it as
I could recall, sat in silence, not uttering a word, not even blinking
an eye. When I finished, he remained mute, weeping heartily. Then
he sent me off to rest and eat, which I did with great enthusiasm. In
the evening, he summoned and addressed me with true generosity
of spirit, exhorting me to make a proper confession, which would
not be too arduous a task, as I had more or less confessed already,
and God would then show us how to proceed. And so I did. The
saintly man said to me, I must admit that your tale does kindle
certain doubts. My Lord, I said, I grant that it is so, and if you wish
to have a matron verify my account, Your Illustrious Lordship, I
shall accept. He said, I am pleased to hear this and shall have it
done. Two old women examined me and were satisfied, declaring
under oath before the bishop that they had found me not only to be
a woman but also a virgin, as immaculate as the day I was born.
I don't know how this could have been, but so it was, as God or
the Virgin wished it. Or both, for it was so. The bishop stood and
embraced me, moved, and declared, My daughter, now I believe

without a shadow of a doubt what you have said; I regard you as one of the most extraordinary persons in this world, and I vow to assist you and attend to your well-being in service to God.

Within a week, His Illustriousness had me sent to the convent of Santa Clara de Guamanga, as there was no other in that city. I donned the veil, aunt, thirty years later. I had to walk beside the bishop, for a great crowd had gathered; not a soul was left who had not come to see me, and so we stalled considerably on our way. Life had wrested me from the labyrinth of cards and drink and daggers and the Reaper, shutting behind me the door I most vigorously longed to never cross again. Yet I was so tired, dear aunt, so spent of strength, that I didn't even think to escape; so dearly did I dread ensnarement by the selfsame trap of the past ten years that I preferred to lock myself away in the very first place where the Reaper had never pursued me: a convent. How it was they found me to be a maid, dear aunt, is a mystery indeed. It must have been another miracle of the Virgin of the Orange Grove. I cannot lie to you, my dearest; there was nothing maidenly about my person, as several of the sisters who received me with delight on that first day would come to learn, and with even greater delight on the days that followed. His Lordship embraced me and blessed me and I went in. They led me to the choir in procession and there I prayed. I kissed the hand of the lady abbess, embraced and was embraced in turn by the nuns. I exchanged faint whispers in the ear with several. The news traveled far and wide, much to the astonishment of everyone who had ever seen me, as well as of those who learned before and after of my feats across the Indies. Over the months I spent inside, I prayed and loved. No loss grieved me more than the death of my bishop, whom I dearly missed. What followed, beloved aunt, was another convent, this time in Lima, under the archbishop's protection; meals with the viceroy; great crowds wherever I trod; my liberation, when proof enough returned from Spain that I had not taken my vows; my return to Spain, the king, the counts, the marquises who granted me their favor and found my conversation engrossing; my lieutenant pension; the right to wear my uniform; a brawl in Italy over a matter of honor that prompted so many to join the fray that I seized my chance to flee; the blessing of the pope; my return to America. And there I was, roaming, as I have always loved to do, when I was apprehended in the middle of the jungle for Lord knows what crime I did not commit—the disappearance of a sheriff whose name I did not even know—and sentenced to death, and so began this story I am telling you now, the story of being here inside a tree. If only you could see it, beloved aunt; its enormous trunk is hollow near the ground and courses with cool air even on the most torrid of days, the yvyrá pytá, the girl taught me the name of this tree, as she has taught me the name of nearly everything else in this place. The girl knows things, my dear, she is a wise child. Do you too believe that everything I have lived thus far has led me to where I am? To this jungle, to these girls, to this letter.

"Hey, che, you are tired. Sleep."

She drapes him with the coat of arms. Antonio closes his eyes. Mitākuña and Michī hug him and sing the sweetest song that any ears have ever heard.

36

The light. It fills everything and brims over. He sees leaves, stalks, coiling tendrils, flowers, fruits, birds, monkeys, weasels, little deer. All trembling in the sun. With veins of sun. Points. Auras. Even the shadows. Especially the shadows. All things float in the sun, shot through with sun. There is nothing in the world that isn't in the sun: what exists is a tissue of flesh or wood or insect flesh or water or some such combination in the sun. Like the two jaguar cubs, drawing so close that he can see nothing but their faces. Golden faces. With vicious jaws. But their wispy whiskers, their pink noses. They're tender. And their sparkling spots. Lovely cubs. He reaches out his hand, his hand is sun, to stroke them.

"Chau, Antonio."

"Jajohecha peve, che."

How strange. It's the girls. He'd already heard that the Indians in this jungle could do such things. Turn into animals, trees, mountains, rivers. But not the eyes. They haven't changed. They're still sweet, black, tapered, shining. The little voices. Michī's plump paw grips his finger. A tear trickles from Antonio. Its glimmers blind him.

"Wait for me, I will go with you."

"Nahániri, che."

"Mba'érepa?"

"We are going, Michī. With mama, sy."

"Sy?"

"Yes, you see."

"Jajohecha peve, Antonio."

"Jajohecha peve, Antonio, che."

"Ore rohayjhu."

"Yes, che, we love you."

"Wait for me, I'm coming."

They kiss him on the forehead. And turn away. They've lengthened. What splendid fur they have. And they walk on all fours. With the jaguars' majestic gait. The weight and grace of strength, of speed. They turn to look at him one last time. Of course they're the girls. He wants to stand, to go with them. He can't. He's tethered to the ground. Like a plant, he can only strain sunward. He tries to struggle. Until he understands. And grows upward. There's no other direction. He weeps and his tears glisten in the light. They water him. Burn him. What will become of him without the girls? Who will he be? A tree? He could follow them from up above. Extend a bough to protect them. Toss down vines as they walk so their tracks are hidden. His chest feels warm. Lovely. It's Tekaka and Kuaru. Also in the sun. Maybe he's a tree already. Do trees have chests? Can they feel the heat of the animals that embrace them? He can. Like he can feel Red, who tucks herself into the space between his torso and right arm. The jaguar girls vanish before they've taken ten steps. They become foliage. They must have turned into ferns. Or the jungle has swallowed them. The jungle has no mouth. Or maybe it does. Antonio doesn't know. He doesn't even know what he is. He feels the earth luring him in. As if he were falling. Heavy. But he doesn't fall. The earth speaks. He doesn't understand what it says. But it speaks: the whole of it is saying something. It vibrates. Antonio feels the tension. The earth must have veins and something courses through it, speaking. It has veins. As he does. His are filling with sunlight. Like leaves. He could swear that he's turning as translucent as leaves. As interwoven with the sun as everything. And how else. What could Antonio ever be without the flesh of his flesh, the jungle? Of the earth. There, fragile, like everything living between the earth and sun, so mineral and yet so alive. But it's a different kind of life, he thinks. A life measured in millennia. In the time of gods. His is the time of butterflies, of yvyrás pitás, of surubí fish, of bees, of jaguars, of ticks, of anteaters, of palms, of flies. The time of what can die so readily. The sun is the time of what does not. Only the sun can kill the sun. Antonio doubts, and he forgets. Something pulses painfully. Something hurts. The air grows hotter. The light dims: birds are veiling the sky. They're fleeing. They call, shrill, shriek. In the treetops, the monkeys howl. On earth, all that can flee is darting, crawling, leaping. It's a stampede.

"Fire, Gato, fire."

"March, you fags! Spread the tar and light the torches, you fucking savages."

"Fire, Gato, fire."

"Burn it down, you sons of bitches!"

The captain has managed to summon ten thousand men. More or less. He doesn't know how many. A rumor spread that there's gold beneath the trees. The Spaniards and their American-born confederates come ceaseless as a tide that swells and swells. But what rains down are darts. What opens is the earth, devouring them. With the jaws of beasts, of snakes, of sharp-edged stones. The trees bristle with new thorns. Venomous. They barely graze the gold-seekers. There's a man on a man on a man on a man. The jungle's floor is turning into men. White and brown and black men too. The oldest, most colossal trees wrench out their roots and fling themselves onto the mass of them. Thunderous. The earth shudders. It's woven out of roots. It swells. It fractures. All things shout and moan. And suffer. Bleed. Die. All on the riverbanks. The white men, and all others with them, try to cordon off the bank: that's where the trees with yellow blossoms grow. They enter that fragrance to kill. Some, few, understand it. And turn back. They don't want to. The jungle embraces them. It armors them with wet leaves. Not the others, pressing on. They advance. Falling. Killing. Dying. It's the gold, they tell themselves. And cease caring even for their lives. All things suffer. Save Antonio, who sleeps. And in his dream he keeps writing to his aunt.

You must know, you do know, do you not?—that beneath the earth the trees live another life, a life we cannot see, the life of their roots entwined, a web of trees, separate above but together below. They rise up, one by one, but they sustain each other. I see them because I myself am taking root, I lace myself into them as they lace themselves into me. They speak to me in a wordless language and I understand them, they say that we are here, we are in the sun and the water, a bond between the earth and heavens, the breath of God creating itself and creating us with each passing instant. We are that which creates life between the rocks and the stars. Star and rock incarnate, we are green and trembling. The world was not made in a single week, beloved aunt, it is made and unmade at every moment.

"Michī, do not cry, che."

"Tekaka, Kuaru, Red, Orchid, Milk, Antonio?"

"Go to mama, che."

The girls run into the outstretched arms of a beautiful young woman. Streaked with the paint of war. Red and black. Teeth and claws. Armed. She embraces her daughters. They melt into each other. They form a mountain that becomes a spring, bathing the brush in ferns and hummingbirds and caimans and little blue frogs and they transform once more into two daughters with their mother and roar their jaguar roars. Antonio watches them. And listens to them. As he listens to the trees that labor underground. Drawing water from the river to cover themselves. Regardless they wither. It's fire. The fire that Antonio always feared. It's here, it's coming. The monkeys shriek at it. Red barks.

And now, beloved aunt, the world burns; the fire enters the earth, we strain our roots into the river to flood ourselves, to put it out, to breathe. It is red on black and black on red and we howl, we throw ourselves onto the men, distill the most exquisite poisons. The serpents sequester themselves in the depths of us, bite into us, give us what is theirs. Our roots bristle with their colors and they slither, quiver. And yet I am a man, my dear, I want my sword, my harquebus, my ruthless aim. I must kill as a man does. I ask the jungle to set me free. I ask the forest, the great spirit of the trees, you should see her, aunt, a glittering woman with hair of leaves and a body brown as wood, but made of the flesh and eyes of trees, greener than the mountains of Europe. She caresses me, dear aunt, and does not answer, she embraces us all, this manger that we are, my animals and me. The fire enters the earth through the roots, burns its insides. I burn, beloved, please ask God to forgive my sins. Our Father, pray with me, who art in heaven, hallowed ...

"Antonio!"

The she-jaguar who interrupted him leaps onto an armed man. Antonio hadn't seen him. She kills him as jaguars do: she sinks her fangs into his neck, she shakes him, breaks him. And that's that. The man is done. Jaguars kill mercifully, in an instant. Another leap and her bloody jaws are poised over his face. Antonio pulses, the whole of him, with panic.

"Hey, che, wake up."

"Mitākuña?"

"No, che, the king of Spain I am. Wake up."

"Mitākuña, you came back, sweet girl."

Antonio hugs her. The girl is enormous. Her neck strong as a mountain. She licks his face.

"We are going."

She licks his face again, his hands. She wakes him.

"What is happening, little one?"

"War, che. Come with me. We are all going."

Antonio sits up, clutching his harquebus. Red, Tekaka, and Kuaru bare their teeth. Mitākuña advances toward the lushest depths of the jungle, which opens to receive her and closes behind her. They hear the groans, the crackling. They breathe the smoke. They move deeper in. They reach a turquoise lagoon with a black stone bed. Shot through with dorado fish as hard and sharp as metal. Bronze blades for fins. On the bank, a legion of tree men. Perhaps a thousand, Antonio thinks. He himself is being covered in leaves. Sprouting with blossoms. Wet, all wet. Shrouded in an air of tree.

"Go fight, che. Send these men."

"Yes, my girl, I will."

"Rohayhu, che."

"Rohayhu, Mitākuña, little one."

Antonio shouts and a tongue of tree slips out of him, a wind. All his men and he himself bound for the boughs. The fire. The animals with their mouths charred into a desperate, eternal howl. A carpet of men. The ash. They've killed a piece of jungle. And they're still coming. The river is rising. It rumbles like a storm come to drown the earth entire. It buckles. They glimpse the innards of black rock. The fish flung up in the sudden warp. The jaguars at the crest of the colossal wave. The Indians everywhere. Milk and Orchid have returned, tremendous, leading a herd of wild horses. The tree men behind them. They rise high and higher. And tumble down. And the water returns to the water. With scraps of white men: the Indians kill those who don't drown. The dorado fish slice them. The tree men choke them with their vines. The ones left over run. No more than a hundred. The Indian women corral them. With the help of two she-jaguars, big as ships, they drive them all into a cave. The hill emits a boulder and seals it. There they are, inside. The birds return. The snakes emerge from the bowels of the earth.

The vulture beholds an inert hole. And a heap of blackened food.

"Hey, che, wake up."

Antonio is baffled: it's Mītākuña. On foot and unfurred. Small as ever. She smells of smoke. But he's down on the ground.

"Antonio."

"Mitākuña, the battle."

"We won, che."

"Did we kill them all?"

"Almost all, but not you. You were here."

"No. I fought with the tree men, little one."

"Nahániri. We took care of you."

"Yes."

"Che, I must go."

"What will you do with the ones left alive?"

"We put them in the jungle, they burned. They left it with no water, no shade, no animals. All ash, che."

"Will they die?"

"I do not know, che. Maybe they eat ash."

"Will you take me with you?"

"Nahániri. But I am close to you, che. Always."

A roar rustles the leaves. The birds scatter, shrieking. The snakes slip into the treetops. Antonio can't see her, but it's Michī, small as ever, opening her mouth. Calling to her sister.

"Rohayhu, Michĩ says. And she tells me to hurry. Now I go."

Mitākuña springs onto him. Embraces him hard. Antonio hugs her back. His little girl. Tears stream down. She dries them with a flick of her feline tongue. By the time Antonio can open his eyes, she's on her feet. She looms immense. Sunlike. Jagua-ress. She gives him another lick, and goes. When the foliage has nearly swallowed her, she turns back to look at Antonio: he has burst into blossom. A hummingbird sips at him. The warmth of Kuaru and Tekaka in his canopy, sweet Red curled in the hollow of his roots. The vulture perched in his boughs vanishes into the light of a star that shoots across the midday sky. Mitākuña flashes her fangs. She laughs.

Acknowledgments

My gratitude to *Ayvu Rapyta*, of the Mbyá Guaraní people, the most beautiful origin story I've ever read. I rewrote it with love, respect, admiration, and the hope for its life-sustaining worldview to permeate us all.

To the autobiography of Catalina de Erauso, which is among the origins of this novel. And to some of its paragraphs.

To the crónica of Antonio Pigafetta, for the seafaring passages.

To Susana Thénon, Alejandra Pizarnik, Mary Oliver, José Watanabe, Juan L. Ortiz, Susana Villalba, and Shakira. For casting their light. And for the dancing.

To Miguel de Cervantes and Francisco de Quevedo, for the pleasure of quoting from them.

To Reynaldo Arenas and João Guimarães Rosa, for their *El mundo alucinante* and *Gran Sertón: Veredas*, respectively.

To my editor, Ana Laura Pérez, because this book was written in conversation with her.

To Sandra Pareja, for her trust and insight, and for always taking me out to explore.

To Robin Myers, for her wonderful English translation.

To Paula Rodríguez, for her keen eye and our impromptu dinners.

To Natalia Brizuela, for her generous readings, including the ones she helps me discover.

To Carolina Cobelo, for lovingly reading this manuscript fifty times. And for helping me with Mitãkuña's song.

To Emilio White, who took me to see the jungle as no one else could have.

To Pilar Cabrera, for the tatatiná on the Paraná and for our talks.

To Gabriela Borrelli Azara, for reading, and for the poems and laughter.

To Mariana Zinni, for generously sharing her knowledge with me.

To Laura Pensa, for her knowledge, too. And for the home-made pasta.

To Victoria Patience, for her meticulous feedback and for encouraging me to go to the jungle.

To Iliana Franco, for reviewing and correcting the Guaraní.

To Sylvia Nogueira, for the Latin.

To Mario Castells, for the Yopará world.

To Eider Rodríguez, for the Basque eye.

To Gabriela Fernández, for the training. And the dog park, always.

To Hayao Miyazaki, for the tenderness and beauty in spite of all death.

New Directions Paperbooks — a partial listing

Adonis, Songs of Mihyar the Damascene
César Aira, Ghosts
   An Episode in the Life of a Landscape Painter
Ryunosuke Akutagawa, Kappa
Will Alexander, Refractive Africa
Osama Alomar, The Teeth of the Comb
Guillaume Apollinaire, Selected Writings
Jessica Au, Cold Enough for Snow
Paul Auster, The Red Notebook
Ingeborg Bachmann, Malina
Honoré de Balzac, Colonel Chabert
Djuna Barnes, Nightwood
Charles Baudelaire, The Flowers of Evil*
Bei Dao, City Gate, Open Up
Yevgenia Belorusets, Lucky Breaks
Rafael Bernal, His Name Was Death
Mei-Mei Berssenbrugge, Empathy
Max Blecher, Adventures in Immediate Irreality
Jorge Luis Borges, Labyrinths
   Seven Nights
Coral Bracho, Firefly Under the Tongue*
Kamau Brathwaite, Ancestors
Anne Carson, Glass, Irony & God
   Wrong Norma
Horacio Castellanos Moya, Senselessness
Camilo José Cela, Mazurka for Two Dead Men
Louis-Ferdinand Céline
   Death on the Installment Plan
   Journey to the End of the Night
Inger Christensen, alphabet
Julio Cortázar, Cronopios and Famas
Jonathan Creasy (ed.), Black Mountain Poems
Robert Creeley, If I Were Writing This
H.D., Selected Poems
Guy Davenport, 7 Greeks
Amparo Dávila, The Houseguest
Osamu Dazai, The Flowers of Buffoonery
   No Longer Human
   The Setting Sun
Anne de Marcken
   It Lasts Forever and Then It's Over
Helen DeWitt, The Last Samurai
   Some Trick
José Donoso, The Obscene Bird of Night
Robert Duncan, Selected Poems
Eça de Queirós, The Maias
Juan Emar, Yesterday

William Empson, 7 Types of Ambiguity
Mathias Énard, Compass
Shusaku Endo, Deep River
Jenny Erpenbeck, Go, Went, Gone
   Kairos
Lawrence Ferlinghetti
   A Coney Island of the Mind
Thalia Field, Personhood
F. Scott Fitzgerald, The Crack-Up
Rivka Galchen, Little Labors
Forrest Gander, Be With
Romain Gary, The Kites
Natalia Ginzburg, The Dry Heart
Henry Green, Concluding
Marlen Haushofer, The Wall
Victor Heringer, The Love of Singular Men
Felisberto Hernández, Piano Stories
Hermann Hesse, Siddhartha
Takashi Hiraide, The Guest Cat
Yoel Hoffmann, Moods
Susan Howe, My Emily Dickinson
   Concordance
Bohumil Hrabal, I Served the King of England
Qurratulain Hyder, River of Fire
Sonallah Ibrahim, That Smell
Rachel Ingalls, Mrs. Caliban
Christopher Isherwood, The Berlin Stories
Fleur Jaeggy, Sweet Days of Discipline
Alfred Jarry, Ubu Roi
B.S. Johnson, House Mother Normal
James Joyce, Stephen Hero
Franz Kafka, Amerika: The Man Who Disappeared
Yasunari Kawabata, Dandelions
Mieko Kanai, Mild Vertigo
John Keene, Counternarratives
Kim Hyesoon, Autobiography of Death
Heinrich von Kleist, Michael Kohlhaas
Taeko Kono, Toddler-Hunting
László Krasznahorkai, Satantango
   Seiobo There Below
Ágota Kristóf, The Illiterate
Eka Kurniawan, Beauty Is a Wound
Mme. de Lafayette, The Princess of Clèves
Lautréamont, Maldoror
Siegfried Lenz, The German Lesson
Alexander Lernet-Holenia, Count Luna

Denise Levertov, Selected Poems
Li Po, Selected Poems
Clarice Lispector, An Apprenticeship
  The Hour of the Star
  The Passion According to G.H.
Federico García Lorca, Selected Poems*
Nathaniel Mackey, Splay Anthem
Xavier de Maistre, Voyage Around My Room
Stéphane Mallarmé, Selected Poetry and Prose*
Javier Marías, Your Face Tomorrow (3 volumes)
Bernadette Mayer, Midwinter Day
Carson McCullers, The Member of the Wedding
Fernando Melchor, Hurricane Season
  Paradais
Thomas Merton, New Seeds of Contemplation
  The Way of Chuang Tzu
Henri Michaux, A Barbarian in Asia
Henry Miller, The Colossus of Maroussi
  Big Sur & the Oranges of Hieronymus Bosch
Yukio Mishima, Confessions of a Mask
  Death in Midsummer
Eugenio Montale, Selected Poems*
Vladimir Nabokov, Laughter in the Dark
Pablo Neruda, The Captain's Verses*
  Love Poems*
Charles Olson, Selected Writings
George Oppen, New Collected Poems
Wilfred Owen, Collected Poems
Hiroko Oyamada, The Hole
José Emilio Pacheco, Battles in the Desert
Michael Palmer, Little Elegies for Sister Satan
Nicanor Parra, Antipoems*
Boris Pasternak, Safe Conduct
Octavio Paz, Poems of Octavio Paz
Victor Pelevin, Omon Ra
Fernando Pessoa
  The Complete Works of Alberto Caeiro
Alejandra Pizarnik
  Extracting the Stone of Madness
Robert Plunket, My Search for Warren Harding
Ezra Pound, The Cantos
  New Selected Poems and Translations
Qian Zhongshu, Fortress Besieged
Raymond Queneau, Exercises in Style
Olga Ravn, The Employees
Herbert Read, The Green Child
Kenneth Rexroth, Selected Poems
Keith Ridgway, A Shock

Rainer Maria Rilke
  Poems from the Book of Hours
Arthur Rimbaud, Illuminations*
  A Season in Hell and The Drunken Boat*
Evelio Rosero, The Armies
Fran Ross, Oreo
Joseph Roth, The Emperor's Tomb
Raymond Roussel, Locus Solus
Ihara Saikaku, The Life of an Amorous Woman
Nathalie Sarraute, Tropisms
Jean-Paul Sartre, Nausea
Kathryn Scanlan, Kick the Latch
Delmore Schwartz
  In Dreams Begin Responsibilities
W. G. Sebald, The Emigrants
  The Rings of Saturn
Anne Serre, The Governesses
Patti Smith, Woolgathering
Stevie Smith, Best Poems
  Novel on Yellow Paper
Gary Snyder, Turtle Island
Muriel Spark, The Driver's Seat
  The Public Image
Maria Stepanova, In Memory of Memory
Wislawa Szymborska, How to Start Writing
Antonio Tabucchi, Pereira Maintains
Junichiro Tanizaki, The Maids
Yoko Tawada, The Emissary
  Scattered All over the Earth
Dylan Thomas, A Child's Christmas in Wales
  Collected Poems
Thuan, Chinatown
Rosemary Tonks, The Bloater
Tomas Tranströmer, The Great Enigma
Leonid Tsypkin, Summer in Baden-Baden
Tu Fu, Selected Poems
Elio Vittorini, Conversations in Sicily
Rosmarie Waldrop, The Nick of Time
Robert Walser, The Tanners
Eliot Weinberger, An Elemental Thing
  Nineteen Ways of Looking at Wang Wei
Nathanael West, The Day of the Locust
  Miss Lonelyhearts
Tennessee Williams, The Glass Menagerie
  A Streetcar Named Desire
William Carlos Williams, Selected Poems
Alexis Wright, Praiseworthy
Louis Zukofsky, "A"